"Raider"

M/M Viking Historical Gay First Time Romance

Jerry Cole

© 2016
Jerry Cole

Disclaimer

All rights reserved. No part of this publication may be reproduced, distributed, or transmitted in any form or by any means, including photocopying, recording, or other electronic or mechanical methods, without the prior written permission of the publisher, except in the case of brief quotations embodied in critical reviews and certain other non-commercial uses permitted by copyright law.

This book is intended for adults (18+) only. The contents may be offensive to some readers. It contains graphic language, explicit sexual content, and adult situations. Please do not read this book if you are offended by such content or if you are under the age of 18. All sexually active characters are 18+.

This is a work of fiction. Names, characters, businesses, places, events and incidents are either the products of the author's imagination or used in a fictitious manner & are not to be construed as real. Any resemblance to actual persons, living or dead, or actual events is purely coincidental.

Cover images are licensed through Stockphotosecrets.com, images shown for illustrative purposes only. Any person(s) that may be depicted on the cover are models.

Edition v1.00 (2016.04.24)
http://www.jerrycoleauthor.com

Table of Contents

Table of Contents..3
Chapter One 4
Chapter Two..12
Chapter Three 28
Chapter Four 47
Chapter Five...60
Chapter Six 74
Chapter Seven...88
Chapter Eight 103
Chapter Nine 107
Chapter Ten 112
Chapter Eleven 132
Chapter Twelve...138
Chapter Thirteen 144

Chapter One

The winds of late summer were cool with the approach of fall as they swept off the coast and over the green, dew-laden hills, stirring the yellow meadow buttercups and the white bursts of cow parsley that splashed color across the dales. Scarlet poppies and toadflax grew in the shelter of the hills, and wary sable hares nibbled thistle and heather, their eyes always watching the horizon for the fire-colored flash of an approaching fox.

Mossy, gray stones erupted from the earth in several places— like they'd been dropped there by a careless giant— and Aiden reclined against one, relishing the warmth of the sun and the brisk breeze. Out before him, his sheep wandered over the marshy green. Their coats were still new from their shearing in late spring, bright white and downy as they ambled over the hills and dipped their noses in shallow, brackish ponds scattered across the low places. Aiden, his fire-colored hair curling in the wind, sighed in contentment. He'd always preferred watching the flock to any other chore, though many turned their nose up to it for the tedium. There were days he simply couldn't bear being in town, and the emptiness of the hilly meadows was a balm to his restless and irritable soul. Without it, he was certain he'd have taken a torch to someone's house by now and confirmed exactly what they all thought about him.

The thought displeased him, and he tried to shrug it off, focusing instead on the wood carving he held in his slender, long-fingered hands. Before she died, his mother had said they were artisan's hands. But there were no artisans here to teach him a trade. Only the sheep and the fields, and Aiden would rather have the sheep than the fields, any day. Still, his mother had taught him a little of carving before she departed, and he'd taught himself a little more by practice. The little ornament in his hands didn't serve too much purpose; it was just a round pendant to which he'd added an excess of intricate carved out details, as a way to pass the time while he watched the sheep. He gave another careful twist of his knife to bring out the shape of a flower less than the size of a pea and smiled, pleased with himself.

A shout distracted him from his work, and he put his knife away to look curiously over his rock. The Cadwgan boy, a scrawny, unconfident thing, often pastured his own family's flock near here. Sure enough, just down the hill, Dilwyn Cadwgan was huddling miserably against a rock while two other boys from town laughed and threatened him with his own crook. Aiden sighed in disappointment. Dilwyn was about thirteen, ten years Aiden's junior. He should have been old enough to look after himself and the sheep. But he was too timid— not to mention inclined to be gangly and awkward in appearance. Aiden was sure he would have been for the priesthood if he hadn't been his father's only son. Still, the way the other boys picked on him was unfair.

The two bullies jumped in surprise as a stone struck the boulder next to their heads.

"Hey, get off!" Aiden shouted down at them, coming around his rock with another stone in his hand and his stick at the ready. "Leave him be!"

"Come down and make us, you redheaded bastard!" one of them shouted back. Aiden's cheeks colored with rage, and he fought the compulsion to rush down the hill and smash both of their ugly faces in. Instead, he squinted down at them harder to make out their identities.

"Caddoc Keelan, if your mother hears you've been harassing the neighbors instead of tracking down that goat you lost, she's going to make a rug of your hide!"

The bigger boy swore vibrantly, threw down Dilwyn's staff, and cast one last insult at Aiden's parentage before running off as Aiden slid down the loose scree of the hill, brandishing his stick and hollering dire violence after them. They vanished over the next hill before Aiden reached the bottom, and he let them go, grumbling in irritation.

"You alright, Wyn?" he asked, turning back to the skinny, miserable boy.

"No," Dilwyn replied, scrubbing the tears off his cheeks in humiliation and bending to pick up his stick. "I hate it here."

"Yeah, don't we all? Still, you've got to learn how to defend yourself. They'll just keep kicking you around, otherwise."

Wyn muttered his agreement, not meeting Aiden's eyes. He'd heard it a thousand times before, but Aiden knew from experience that it wasn't as easy as just hearing it. He'd had his fair share of kickings from local bullies.

"I'm sorry they called you a bastard," Dilwyn said. "You didn't have to help me."

"I am a bastard," Aiden said with a shrug. "If I let it bother me, I'd never get any rest."

"Guess that explains why you're such a bitter ass."

Aiden snorted.

"Exactly," he agreed. "And watch your mouth. That's how you get lunk heads like Caddoc after you. Ignorance can't abide wit."

"Thank you, anyway." Dilwyn stood, dusting off his pants. "I'll plug 'em myself next time."

"You had better," Aiden replied. "I won't be around to save you every time. You don't want to end up a bitter ass like me, do you?"

"Nah, that'd be a tragedy."

Aiden followed Dilwyn back up the hill to find his flock. From their spot at the crest of the hill, they could see the little village on the coast below, a brown and miserable muddy splotch against the side of the island. Aiden felt more miserable just looking at it.

"I hate this place," Dilwyn said, hanging on his crook like the weight of unhappiness was dragging him down.

"Might as well get used to it," Aiden said with a sigh. "There isn't anywhere else."

As the day wound down toward afternoon, the two gathered their flocks and headed back toward town where the bells were ringing for evening mass.

Dilwyn's mother met them on their way into town and scolded Wyn for taking so long, hurrying him off to get ready for church. She didn't so much as look at Aiden, but Aiden was used to that. Wyn waved goodbye as they parted, and Aiden drove his flock home alone. The bells rang again as he pulled icy water from the well to wash his face, and for a moment, he considered staying home. But the people around here disliked him enough already. He didn't need to give them further ammunition against him. Better to just get this over with.

    The church was a plain stone building in the center of town, the bell tower its only ornamentation. Despite its austere appearance, it was the largest and most important building in the village, which resided firmly within the iron fist of the village priest, Father Maredudd. The father was a tall, narrow man who resembled nothing so much as an arrow slit in a castle wall, dressed all in black with a pointed head and a sharp gray beard. Humorless as a Welsh winter and twice as cold, Maredudd took his responsibility for the town with grave sobriety, seeing it as his sole burden to steer the otherwise hopelessly wayward villagers toward salvation. He took the metaphor of shepherd steering his flock quite seriously, in that he believed with certainty that everyone in this town was as brainless as your average sheep and doomed unless threatened by heavy sticks and the hounds of hell snapping at their heels. For all his faith in the Lord, Maredudd had precious little faith in humanity.

    Aiden sat on a splintery wooden pew near the back of the chapel as Father Maredudd gave his service, hoping to avoid notice by the priest— or anyone else, if he could help it. Mass was a daily affair in the village, and missing it too many times could result in fines or public chastisement, administered by Maredudd with a heavy pine rod. Aiden had felt the sting of that rod more than once, and he didn't fancy meeting it again. As long as he was seen in attendance and otherwise kept his head down, he could look forward to a life of being left to his own devices— a life which was long and lonely and under constant scrutiny by every other fool in this town. The thought made Aiden want to crawl into his bed and never leave it, or else go sprinting across the hills, shrieking, and never look back. But he wasn't suicidal, and he knew there was nowhere else out there for him that held anything better. This was the life the God of a man like Maredudd would saddle a person like him with, and he simply had to accept it.

Having finished the ritualized portion of mass, Maredudd began his sermon, to which Aiden did his best to pay no attention.

"Heed, my children, the words of Leviticus! The man that committeth adultery with another man's wife— even he that committeth adultery with his neighbor's wife— the adulterer and the adulteress shall surely be put to death. Heed also this of Deuteronomy! A bastard shall not enter into the congregation of the Lord! Even to his tenth generation shall he not enter into the congregation of the Lord!"

Aiden ducked his head lower as Maredudd began on one of his favorite subjects. There were three things that worried Maredudd excessively. More than any other sin, he feared idolaters, adulterers, and their offspring. Aiden, as such, was not very popular with the Father.

"Guard well your chastity, my children," the Father intoned, his voice ringing in the high stone ceiling. "Give in not to fleeting temptation. The fruits of the flesh are meager and bitter on the tongue, and the repercussions are dire beyond measure not just for yourself, but for all your seed..."

Aiden squared his shoulders and bore through it by the power of pure spite. *Whine and mutter all you like, Maredudd*, he thought. *You couldn't keep me out. I'm still here, and I'm not going anywhere, much as I might like to.*

Mass ended, and the congregation trickled out of the building and out into the early evening air. Aiden took a moment to just stand in the cool of it, staring up at the silver stars just coming into view above them. A few of the more friendly townsfolk nodded to him or said a quick greeting, which he returned. No need to sour the few relationships he had that weren't actively antagonistic. Old Gethin the blacksmith gave him a brief smile, and Aiden, surprised, smiled back. Briallen Pritchard followed directly behind him with a disgusted scowl, like Aiden was a diseased dog who'd wandered into her Christmas dinner. The brief happiness he'd felt at Gethin's approval deflated abruptly.

Home was a small house on the edge of village— empty now, since his father had died a few winters back. Most of the other houses in the village housed whole families: grandparents and cousins and more. Aiden lived alone, and tried to tell himself he preferred it that way. But at night, lying in bed with the silence of the house like a smothering blanket around him, he longed to be anywhere else. He didn't care where, so long as there was someone there who was happy to see him.

Chapter Two

Much to his surprise, bells woke him the next morning. He climbed out of bed and pulled on his clothes, stumbling out into the sunlight to see what had happened. It wasn't the church bells, but the town bell, which was generally only used for important announcements or emergencies. People were gathering by the town well in front of the church, including the town's nominal leader, Gaenor Pugh. Pugh stood beside Maredudd, looking anxiously down the road into town. The Rhodri boy stood near them, presumably having run from the Rhodri farm, which was just down that way and something of a watch post for the town.

The late summer morning air was already heavy with warmth, and the drone of fat bees that ambled through the flowering heather beside the road. The sky was a brilliant sapphire, scattered with wooly white clouds, and high above, a falcon was wheeling, searching for prey on the moor. Up the dusty road into town a group of men was walking, pulling a hand cart.

Aiden joined the other townsfolk by the well, and as the group grew nearer, he saw why everyone was concerned. The men were all tall and broad-chested, with thick, neatly-kept beards and weapons on their hips. The words 'northmen' drifted through the crowd of villagers, a frightened whisper. They'd all heard the rumors of heathens from the north raiding monasteries and villages along the coast. But surely if they planned to attack, Aiden thought, they wouldn't be coming up the road so calmly?

"Hale," one called— a huge man with hair only a shade darker than Aiden's— "We're looking to trade. Do you have supplies for sale or barter?"

Pugh looked at Maredudd questioningly, both of them clearly wary of the northmen. Maredudd shook his head, always against interacting with heathens.

"We have silver!" the redheaded man called again, holding up a hefty coin purse.

"Welcome!" Pugh held out his arms at once, moving forward to invite the strangers in. "We have supplies for travelers. What all do you need? Come, we'll talk and arrange everything."

The redheaded leader and two other men followed Pugh and Maredudd off to talk trade, while the other man stood awkwardly back, watching the villagers watching them.

One of the men was a tall, fair-haired man, not too much older than Aiden, by his looks. His eyes were the blue gray of a sky before rain, and his features were roughhewn, but handsome. He saw Aiden staring and returned his glance with a polite nod. Aiden risked a smile. Dangerous as these men looked, it didn't seem like they'd come in search of trouble, and the trade might be good for the town. The blond man returned the smile with a slightly amused one of his own. He turned suddenly, leaving his group to approach Aiden. Aiden froze, realizing he'd accidentally invited conversation.

"That amulet," the man said, gesturing to the wooden token around Aiden's neck. "It looks finely crafted. Was it made here?"

Aiden touched the carved medal in surprise. It was the one he'd been working on the day before, and he flushed a little with unexpected happiness at the compliment.

"Aye. By me," he replied, wary despite the flattery.

The man seemed impressed, maintaining an easy, friendly air, his confidently casual attitude somehow the most intimidating thing about him.

"Do you have any others you'd be willing to trade?" he asked. "I've got a little girl back home who'll skin me alive if I don't bring something back for her."

Aiden laughed a little, caught off guard by the other man's humor.

"I do," he agreed, deciding maybe it was worth it to give the man a chance. "Give me just a second to go and get them."

By the time he returned with a collection of his carvings, the other villagers had warmed up and were talking to the strangers as well, trading and haggling easily.

He knelt on the grass to spread out the handful of little woodwork he'd brought out, and the man reached at once for a delicate token featuring a design of a bird tangled in flowering briar.

"She'd love this one," he said, running his fingers over the details. "Birds are her favorite. I like the one you're wearing best myself, but I think this is the one. What'll you take for it? Silver?"

"I don't trade," Aiden shook his head, settling back on the grass. "I've got no use for silver."

"What do you have use for?" the man asked, sitting down across from him and leaning forward with interest. "Wood, perhaps? I've got a stack of good lumber back at our camp."

"I've got plenty of wood," Aiden said with a shrug. "If all you've got is pine, I don't need it."

"Ever carved with lime wood?" The man leaned on his hands, smiling at Aiden like he was enjoying the conversation. "I'm told its quite pleasant to work with."

Aiden couldn't hide his sudden interest.

"I haven't," he confessed. "I only do this to pass the time when I'm watching the sheep. I'll take that, then. Five good pieces, about this size."

He gestured with his hands to indicate what he wanted, and the man scoffed.

"It's a pretty trinket," the man said. "But it's not that pretty. I'll give you half a log that size."

"Is a little wood worth disappointing your daughter and losing your skin?" Aiden crossed his arms stubbornly. "Four pieces."

"Two, and not a scrap more," the man said. "And only because I like your art and I want to encourage it. Artists like you shouldn't have to be herding sheep."

Aiden probably could have haggled another log out of the man, but the compliment caught him off guard, and he blushed as he tried to recover.

"I'm no artist. It's just a pastime."

"There's no carpenter in a village this small, is there?" The man took a guess. Aiden just shrugged.

"You ought to try another town." The stranger bent to catch Aiden's eye, looking at him seriously. "There's one down the coast with a carpenter that might take you. You've got the talent for it."

Aiden felt a weird hope fluttering in his chest, like a lopsided bird, trying and failing to take off.

"I can't," he said at last. "I've got the house to look after, and the sheep."

The man seemed to realize he was being presumptuous and sat back, hands up.

"Forgive me; I shouldn't be sticking my nose in. I'm sure you've got a family to be taking care of."

"No," Aiden admitted, turning a carving over in his hands. "It's just me and the sheep."

The man frowned, seemingly at a loss, and after a moment, Aiden shook it off and smiled.

"I'll take it," he said, offering his hand. "Two pieces, and you throw in one of those beads from your beard. To remember you by."

The man's eyes widened, and he gave a sudden low laugh, reaching out to shake Aiden's hand.

"It's a deal. Give me a moment to fetch your lumber."

The man stood, turning for the cart the strangers had brought with them, then paused.

"My name is Einarr," he said, his smile warm.

"Aiden," the smaller man replied, pleased by the conversation.

"A pleasure to meet you, Aiden." Einarr tipped his head to Aiden briefly, then strode off to the cart, digging out the wood he'd promised.

While they'd been talking, Pugh and the redheaded leader seemed to have come to an agreement. They emerged from Pugh's house, shaking hands, and the redheaded man clapped Pugh on the back hard enough to make the smaller man stumble before he headed back to his cart. He spoke to the other men briefly, including Einarr, and they prepared to leave. Einarr jogged back across the square to offer Aiden two sizeable pieces of soft, pale wood.

"There you are," he said, handing them over. "And this."

He pulled a thumbnail-sized blue bead from one of his braids as Aiden set the wood aside and offered a smile. Aiden took it, turning it admiringly in the light, then tucked it into his pocket, handing over the bird carving.

"Agni is going to love this." Einarr admired the carving for a moment before tucking it away.

"Here, take this too," Aiden said after a moment, pulling the token Einarr had admired over his head and holding it out. "As a gift."

Einarr looked caught off guard for a moment, but then, he took the little amulet and hung it around his neck.

"Thank you, Aiden." He patted the younger man on the shoulder, obviously touched, and said, "I'll be back tomorrow to pick up the supplies your town sold us. Perhaps I'll see you then?"

"I'd like that," Aiden agreed, his stomach fluttering strangely at the thought of seeing the man again.

They said their goodbyes, and Aiden watched the strangers vanish down the road, already eagerly anticipating their return. A part of him insisted it was foolish to be getting so excited about a bunch of traders. They'd be gone by tomorrow afternoon, likely for good. But he couldn't help the warmth that blossomed in his chest at the thought that someone, anyone, was looking forward to seeing him again.

He took the pale lime wood out to the fields with the sheep and started a new carving to replace the one he'd given Einarr. The wood was soft, easy on his knife, but firm enough to hold details. He'd have to try and find more of it in the future. Traders and merchants didn't stop in this town often, small and out of the way as it was. Perhaps that town down the coast would have it... He didn't need to move there; maybe he could visit every once in a while, just to buy wood. Without really noticing, he'd carved Einarr's likeness into the wood. He considered showing the man tomorrow, then dismissed the idea quickly, blushing. No, he would keep this one to himself.

That night, he laid in bed and watched the moonlight through his window as it crawled slowly over his wall. He couldn't stop thinking about the traders— Einarr, especially. The blond man's smile lingered in Aiden's mind, despite all efforts to forget it. He rolled over to stare at the blue bead sitting on the table near his bed, shining softly in the moonlight. He wondered where those men were camping and where they were heading to. Perhaps, if he asked, they'd be willing to take him with them— at least as far as that town down the coast. Einarr had been right; Aiden didn't have anything keeping him here but memories. He should have left ages ago. He'd been so resigned to misery that he'd never really considered leaving an option. But then again, no one but his own mother had ever said his carving was skillful enough to make a career of. In another place, no one would know of his uncertain parentage. He'd be no more alone than he was here, and perhaps he'd even be able to make friends. It was a foolish thought. He was asking for trouble, but the hope persisted as he tossed and turned through the night, kept awake by the first genuine anticipation he'd felt since before his father's death.

    The next morning, he woke early to tend his garden and check on his sheep quickly, getting it out of the way before morning bells so he'd be certain not to miss the arrival of the strangers when they came for their supplies. Men were already carrying out the crates and sacks to the road as he finished up and went to the well to wash up. As Aiden bent over in his garden, Einarr's bead fell from his pocket. He crouched to retrieve it with a frown of irritation and was about to straighten up when he heard voices approaching the well.

"And you're certain it's right with the Lord?"

Aiden recognized the voice of Pugh and started to stand and greet the man, but his voice was lowered surreptitiously, and the reason why came a second later as Father Maredudd replied.

"The Lord God despises heathen unbelievers," Maredudd said with self-righteous solemnity. "He does not extend them the protection he bestows on his children. And furthermore, it may be that these are the same northmen that ravaged the monastery at Lindisfarne not so long ago. In which case, this would be the least of the punishments they deserve."

Aiden froze, dread creeping into his veins like cold water. Were Pugh and Maredudd planning to attack the traders? Surely not even they could be that foolish. It was more likely they were simply planning to cheat them.

"We've made the tops of the barrels to look like they're full of good supplies," Pugh said, confirming Aiden's suspicions, as the man bent to wash his face and drink from the well. "They shouldn't notice they've been shorted at least until they've left."

"Fear not, my friend," Maredudd reassured him. "The Lord is with us in this righteous act of justice against his heathen enemies."

Aiden stayed hidden beside the well until the two men had wandered off, sudden guilt gnawing at his gut. He didn't care what Maredudd said; cheating the traders was wrong— but on the other hand, it was only some supplies. It wasn't likely they'd die without them. And telling them would mean putting everyone in his village in danger of the strangers' retribution. What if they really were the northmen who'd taken Lindisfarne? He'd heard there were rapes at Lindisfarne, and young men— monastic apprentices— carried off into slavery. And cruel deaths. Monks stripped naked and shoved out into the cold, drowned in the sea, or burned inside their homes. He felt sick with fear imagining it. He didn't believe Einarr with his kind smile could have done something like that. The others hadn't looked that cruel, either. There was no way they could be responsible. They were just travelers in need of supplies. They didn't deserve to be robbed for that. But what could he do? He certainly couldn't control Pugh and Maredudd's actions. Maredudd already hated him, and the mayor took the priest's advice in nearly all things. This would be all the excuse they needed to drive him out, most likely with only the clothes on his back and whatever injuries they could justify adding to his punishment. Aiden returned to his work, chewing his lip with worry and indecision.

    Less than an hour later, the Rhodri boy came running down the road to let them know the traders were on their way. Soon, they could be seen coming up the road, hauling their cart again, which was now empty to carry back their supplies. Aiden stood to the side of the square as they approached, exchanging cheerful greetings. The red-bearded leader handed over the agreed upon weight of silver in both coins and scrap, then began helping his men load the barrels and crates into their cart. As they were working, Aiden spotted Einarr, who raised a hand to wave at him cheerfully. Aiden felt his guilt growing painfully within him as he waved back, his expression grim. Einarr frowned, sensing something was wrong. Aiden couldn't help himself from glancing down at the barrel in Einarr's hands. Einarr followed his gaze, frowning, and shifted the barrel, weighing it thoughtfully. Whatever he felt made his frown deepen. He leaned over to his leader, whispering something in his ear. The red haired man scowled.

"The men say the barrels are light," he said in a loud, clear voice, making Pugh, who'd been carrying the silver, quickly back to his house, freeze, and turn back.

"You aren't cheating us, are you?"

"Of course not!" Pugh said immediately. "Such treachery would be an abomination in the eyes of God."

"Aye. It'd be an abomination to our Gods as well." The redheaded man took the light barrel from Einarr's hands. "So then you won't mind if we check the goods?"

"Of course not!" Pugh's voice shook, and sweat glistened on his pale forehead. "Everything is in order; you'll see."

The redheaded man set the barrel on the ground and pulled the top off. At first, Pugh looked relieved as a layer of glistening red apples greeted them, piled up the very edge of the barrel. But the strangers' leader looked unconvinced. He plunged his hand into the barrel, scattering apples as he reached down past what he could see. With a disgusted sound, he pulled up a moldering old fruit from last winter and a fistful of hay. Beneath the top layer, which was perhaps a pound of healthy fruit, there was nothing but straw and apples too old and shriveled to feed to anything but hogs.

"You planted that," Pugh said quickly. "You're just trying to get more out of us!"

At once, the villagers took up a call of agreement, several of them reaching for weapons. The strangers, meanwhile, were opening more crates and barrels, exclaiming in a strange, blunt-sounding language Aiden didn't recognize as they discovered more of the same in every one: a thin layer of genuine goods followed by hay and moldy refuse.

"If you would so ungraciously attempt to swindle these good Christian men, then you had best take your tainted silver and be gone." Father Maredudd's nose was in the air with contempt as he stood beside Pugh. Pugh hugged the sack of silver more tightly.

"Keep it," the redheaded man spat, then said something in his native tongue that sounded distinctly like a curse. He barked something at his men, who unloaded the false goods, flinging them at Pugh's feet, then turned and left. Aiden watched them go, hope crumbling as Einarr refused to even look at him. He looked at Pugh, his disgust undisguised as Pugh smugly clutched his winnings and Maredudd looked on with sanctimonious righteousness, as though he had thwarted some great evil rather than just cheating and being caught by a group of honest traders. Overwhelmed by anger and frustration at what they'd done, Aiden hurried away, fetching his sheep and heading out to the hills— worried if he didn't, he might swing his crook at Maredudd's head like a club.

He returned in the evening, calmer, but no less sick at heart. He wouldn't stay here another night after this. He was leaving tomorrow, even if he had to go alone. He packed up his things, carefully wrapping all of his carvings and the lime wood, hoping it might find him a job wherever he was going. He'd sell his sheep, probably to the Cadwgan's, in exchange for the money and supplies he'd need to travel. The bead from Einarr, he tucked into his pocket after a last admiring glance. At least he would have that to remember who had inspired him to do this— to try and find a life he could enjoy, living rather than one he could simply survive.

Darkness had just fallen, and he had just finished packing— ready to leave in the morning— when the town bell began ringing, loud and frantic. He frowned in confusion, setting aside his bag and reaching for his crook. The bell ringing this late at night could only be trouble. A fire, or someone stealing sheep, perhaps. He hurried out of his door just as the ringing of the bell cut off abruptly; someone had struck its ringer in the face with an ax. All the buildings on the north end of town were burning, and by their hellish light, Aiden could see the traders they'd betrayed; their numbers had tripled now, and they were making their way through the streets, moving systematically from house to house, killing occupants, taking what they wanted, and then setting the structure ablaze. The bell had woken the villagers and, panicked and disorganized, they fled from the fire, most of them directly into the arms of waiting northmen with axes. Aiden clutched his crook and ran out, knowing he'd only be trapped if he stayed in his home. He saw the Rhodri boy run past him to the church. Dilwyn Cadwgan was kneeling in the street next to his father, who was most certainly dead, though Dilwyn, with desperate sobs, kept trying to wake him.

"The church!" Pugh ran past him, holding his infant daughter. "Get the children to the church!"

Aiden grabbed Dilwyn under the arms and hauled the boy to his feet, dragging him away from his father's corpse and toward the stone building. The Rhodri boy joined them, and Aiden pushed them both into Pugh's hands on the church steps.

"I'll keep looking!" Pugh shouted as he slammed the church doors and turned, running back toward the houses. "Guard them!"

A pit of hollow fear opened in Aiden's stomach as he clutched his wooden staff, knowing it would be nothing against steel axes and swords. But he held his ground, his eyes round and white with fear as the northmen, done looting that side of town, advanced toward him.

"There's nothing but children in here!" he shouted as they drew closer, hands shaking as he held out his stick. "Take what you want elsewhere! You don't need them!"

"Don't bother lyin' to us, boy." A man with dark hair and a heavy ax strode toward him unhurriedly, the others behind him. "You sheep folk always keep your best treasures in your churches."

He tried to shove Aiden aside, not caring enough to kill him. Aiden, panic burning in his veins, swung his staff at the man as hard as he could. It splintered into shards over the man's head. The man, who was at least six feet tall, turned slowly to look at Aiden, murder in his eyes.

"Just leave them alone!" Aiden half-shouted, half-sobbed, brandishing the shattered stump of his staff. "Just take what you want and go!"

"Oh, I'm going to take what I want," the man growled, and his friends laughed as he hefted his ax and stepped toward Aiden. Aiden gripped what was left of his stick and braced himself. Everything had happened so fast and there was so much chaos, he wasn't even really thinking about the fact that he was about to die. He just couldn't let them in. He had to protect the children.

The man swung at him, and Aiden quickly threw himself out of the way with a shout, hitting the ground and rolling away from another strike, directly into the kick of one of the other men. He rolled back, wheezing as the air was knocked out of him. His attacker stopped swinging long enough to laugh at Aiden, blue in the face and coughing as he tried to get his air back. But Aiden was still clutching his splintered stick, and he climbed unsteadily to his feet with it, holding his gut with his other hand.

"Just... go..." he wheezed. "Please."

"I'm going to have fun beating the fire out of you," the man laughed.

"Hold just a moment there, Branulf."

The familiar voice caught Aiden off guard and he looked around, confused, as Einarr appeared out of the dark. Aiden felt his heart breaking at the sight of the other man participating in this. Somehow, he'd hoped Einarr at least wouldn't do this.

"Leave that one be," Einarr was saying. "I want him."

"We're not taking slaves today, Einarr," Branulf argued, put out.

"I don't want to sell him," Einarr replied. "I want him for my thrall. He reminds me of Bard."

"Mmm... Bard did have that same stubborn way of not knowing when he was beaten," Branulf conceded with an irritated sigh and stepped back. "Fine, take the boy if you want him. I just want whatever is in that church."

The men stepped aside as Einarr approached, and Aiden readied himself, holding the broken end of his staff out in front of him. Fear and disappointment battled within him.

"They haven't done anything to you," Aiden shouted, furious and terrified. "It wasn't their fault!"

"Sorry for this, friend," Einarr said casually, pulling a club from his belt. "You'll thank me for this later."

Aiden ran at him, angry tears in his eyes, and Einarr struck him hard across the temple. Darkness swallowed him up, and the last thing he saw was the fire as it engulfed the home he'd lived in all his life.

Chapter Three

Aiden woke briefly in the early dawn light with rough wood under his cheek. He groaned and struggled to sit up, his head swimming, and saw the shore retreating behind them, pale blue in the morning haze. He felt a confused panic rising within him, but his head swam and throbbed in time with his heartbeat, making darkness crowd the edges of his vision. A gentle hand patted his head, easing him back down to the bottom of the boat.

"Just rest now, boy; no need to get yourself worked up. Just rest."

Though he wanted to resist that hand, to leap to his feet, jump from this boat and swim home, unconsciousness fell on him like a smothering blanket, and he drifted into darkness again.

When he next woke, there was sun on his face and rope around his wrists.

"He's a bit skinny, but I'd give you eight ounces of silver for him."

Aiden opened his eyes and stirred against the rough, unvarnished wood he was lying on, his head throbbing as he tried to get his bearings.

"I'm afraid that one's not for sale. But let us talk about that cheese you have there."

Aiden recognized Einarr's voice and turned his head to try and see the man, jumping when he realized someone was watching him. Branulf, the huge man who'd challenged him in front of the church, was sitting near him in the otherwise empty boat, watching him. Aiden flinched away at first, but the man just yawned, bored, and glanced away over the sea. The boat he was in— a long, shallow, wooden vessel— was pulled up onto the sand of a shore Aiden didn't recognize. Two other boats were pulled up alongside it, and a host of men— sixty or seventy— milled about the shore, relaxing and stretching their legs. Einarr was only a few feet away, talking with a Moorish trader.

"Ten ounces, then," the trader pushed, "And I will give you the cheese for free. This is more than a fair price."

Aiden paled, suddenly unsure if he was more afraid of being sold or staying here. At least he had spoken with Einarr and had some concept of the man's character. He shot Branulf a wary look, but the man said nothing to reassure him, more interested in the splinter he was picking off the side of the ship.

"Sorry, friend," Einarr answered the man. "It's a very fair price. But I'm afraid that one is mine. I don't intend to sell him at any price."

"Ah, pity," the trader said while Aiden breathed a sigh of relief. "That hair color is quite popular in the east. If you tire of him before he's spent, he'd still fetch a decent price there."

"I'll keep it in mind," Einarr assured him. "Now, about that cheese."

He haggled with the trader a little longer while Aiden contemplated his bonds. The rope around his hands was knotted around the mast of the ship. Even with a knife, he didn't think he could get through the rope before Branulf or the others noticed. And even if he did, his only escape would be to sprint inland— he had no idea where he was or what the terrain was like. If there were forest beyond this rocky coast, he might hide, but if there were only hills, he'd be doomed.

While he was debating this, Einarr finished his conversation and returned to the boat, smiling when he saw Aiden sitting up.

"Oh, good, you're awake." Einarr tossed what he'd bought into the boat and climbed in after it, then knelt before Aiden, grabbing the younger man by the chin and turning his face so that Einarr could see where he'd hit him with the club. "How is your head feeling?"

It hurt, but Aiden said nothing, lips pressed tightly together at the indignity of being handled that way. How could he ask that, Aiden wondered, after he was the one who'd hit Aiden in the first place? Einarr seemed to pick up on Aiden's agitation after a moment and nodded, letting him go.

"I think your new wife is angry with you," Branulf said with a chuckle, and Einarr frowned at the other man, then shrugged, letting it go.

"Well, I suppose I would be as well, wouldn't I?" He patted Aiden's head, carefully avoiding the spot where he'd hit him. "He'll warm up to me in time."

"I wouldn't count on it." Branulf leaned back, putting his feet up, "Redheads are always too willful."

Einarr was digging through the things he'd brought and scoffed at Branulf as the other man reclined with his eyes closed, ready for a nap in the sun.

"You're only still bitter because he hit you." He pulled a hunk of bread and cheese from the bag. "Don't tell me you're not. You've been all scowls since last night."

"Not for that little flea bite!" Branulf said indignantly. "It's that damn church I'm sore about. Not a thing worth having in it but a pack of squalling bairns."

"Did you hurt them?" Aiden spoke at last, staring holes into Branulf. "Did you hurt the children?"

Branulf opened his eyes to give Aiden an insulted look.

"There's no honor in fighting children," he responded after a moment. "Why bother?"

The tension drained from Aiden's shoulders as relief washed over him. At least they were safe. Whatever else happened, he'd accomplished that much.

"Well, at least he's still capable of talking," Einarr sighed with relief. "Even if it's only to you, Branulf. I was starting to worry I'd knocked the sense out of him. Here, boy, you've been asleep for nearly a day. You must be thirsty."

Einarr offered Aiden a flask and a piece of the bread and cheese. Aiden briefly considered throwing it overboard in protest, but he was hungry and couldn't abide wastefulness besides. So he accepted the meal silently and ate, still refusing to speak to Einarr— or even look at him, if he could help it.

"You know, you will have to speak to me eventually," Einarr said. "You're going to be living with me. It'd be an awful shame to have a silent companion."

"Agni makes enough noise for the both of you," Branulf laughed. "Give me a bit of that cheese, will you?"

"Get your own," Einarr replied with good humor. "Arnnjorn is insisting I've got to buy the boy's food with my own money. He won't let me pull it from the supplies."

"As he should," Branulf nodded in agreement, reaching for the cheese himself. "We didn't supply for carrying thralls."

"Yes, he's within his rights." Einarr smacked Branulf's hand away. "But that doesn't mean I've got to feed you as well."

"Stingy," Branulf grumbled, but let it be, going back to his nap. Aiden was still eating his food, quiet and pensive as he considered what he would do to get out of this. Perhaps, if he cooperated, they would untie him at one of their next stops and he'd be able to make a break for it. He just needed to bide his time and keep his eyes open for a chance.

"Einarr!" A huge, red-bearded man— which Aiden recognized as the men's leader— wandered past. "You finish getting what you need for that new pet of yours?"

"Once I convinced that merchant I wasn't selling him, yes." Einarr was smiling, his tone light and conversational as ever. "He thought I was denying him just to drive up the price."

"As long as it's done," the other man waved Einarr off casually. "We need to get back under sail. We can make it far further down the coast today."

"Are we in such a hurry, Arnnjorn?" Branulf asked, cracking an eye curiously.

"Mark the wind." Arnnjorn tipped his head to the north, where a chill in the air made the bright day pleasant. "End of summer is coming. I want to be home in time to get the harvest in. With the supplies we got from the village, we should be able to make it back without having to stop more than once or twice more. We could be back in three days with favorable wind."

"Three days?" Branulf repeated, incredulous. "You are missing your bed."

"Yes, and I'm also in charge, so you'll do as I say," Arnnjorn said, only half seriously. But still, Einarr stood up, stretching, and Branulf followed him with a muttered complaint. Einarr ruffled Aiden's hair as they went to gather up the rest of the men, who crowded back into the boats, stowing their supplies and belongings in a small space under the deck. Einarr took a seat beside Aiden, keeping the boy close to his side as the ship was pushed off of the sand and back out into the cold sea.

Aiden had never been to sea before, at least not that he remembered, though he supposed he must have sailed with his mother when they'd come back with his father. He found the rocking not unpleasant and the view agreeable, but having to share the space with so many people— all of whom had been involved in the destruction and murder of everything and everyone he'd ever known— somewhat spoiled the adventure. And it was Einarr he was angriest at, despite being huddled against his side this way, because Einarr had dared to try and be his friend first, and then attempted to act like nothing had happened after. To do such a thing and then smile at Aiden that way afterward, the man must be a monster.

When the wind died, or was simply too slow for Arnnjorn's liking, they pulled out oars and one was shoved into Aiden's hands as well. He stared at it blankly for a moment until Einarr suddenly leaned closer behind him. Aiden tensed with surprise as the man's chest pressed against his back while Einarr took Aiden's hands.

"Here, it's like this," he explained, moving Aiden's hands to the right place and guiding him in putting the oar in the water. "Just follow what the man in front of you is doing. Try to stay in rhythm with him. Can you do it?"

He was so close, Aiden could feel the man's breath, warm on his ear, and he nodded quickly just to make Einarr let him go. He didn't know why it flustered him so much to have the man's arms around him like that. He blamed it on agitation about how the man had betrayed him and tried to focus on rowing the way Einarr had showed him. It was worth it just to have something else to focus on besides Einarr being so close to him. He was suddenly all too aware of how close the larger man was to him, and he didn't care for it. He would have fled to put some distance between them if there was any space to be had on this boat. But somehow, he didn't think being cuddled up with Branulf or Arnnjorn would be any better.

As night fell, his arms aching from the rowing, Aiden found himself dozing off against Einarr's shoulder, unable to help the way his heavy head fell against the older man's side. Einarr put an arm around him, warm and secure, and Aiden was too tired to resist, falling asleep to the sound of the other man humming an old, soothing song.

He woke when the man moved the next morning as, in the gray early morning light, they dragged the ship up onto the sand again. Aiden's wrists were sore, chafed by the rope, and his legs ached from sitting so long. As the other men climbed out of the boat, Aiden realized he couldn't keep up his policy of silence much longer. He reached out as Einarr stood, catching the other man's sleeve.

"Could I," he muttered, quiet with embarrassment, "Could I get up? Please?"

He tacked the please on, though it embarrassed him, hoping it would earn him a little more favor with the older man. It seemed to work, as Einarr smiled and reached over to untie the end of his rope from the mast.

"There," he said, tying it to his own belt instead. "You can follow me around while I work."

Aiden scowled at the rope, clearly not pleased by this turn of events.

"Unless you'd prefer to wait in the boat?" Einarr reached for the rope as though he planned to retie it to the mast again, and Aiden reached out quickly to stop him.

"Thank you," he said instead, quick and bitter and lacking sincerity.

Einarr, pleased, helped Aiden step out of the boat and made his way up the beach with Aiden following along behind him, sullen and unhappy. But this still might be his chance, he thought, looking at the scrubby pine forest beyond the beach. If he could get loose long enough to dart into those woods, he might have a chance. He just needed to get loose of his ropes first. He began twisting his sore, raw wrists, trying to loosen the rope's grip on him enough to pull his hands through. He hadn't been at it long, however before Einarr finished stretching and led him off to where Arnnjorn was standing, watching the men pull the third boat up onto the sand.

"What do you need done, Arnnjorn?" Einarr asked of the huge man.

"You have something caught on your trousers there, Einarr," Arnnjorn said, eyeing Aiden critically.

"Couldn't keep him in the boat the whole trip," Einarr said with a shrug. "If his legs wither off before we get home, he'll be useless."

"No man's legs ever withered off in four days."

"He might be the first, skinny as he is. I'd rather not find out."

Arnnjorn shook his head, clearly baffled by Einarr's attachment to the English boy, but finally answered Einarr's question.

"This place is good for lumber, and there's fruit a little further inland," he said. "Take a few men and go see what you can find. Be back before midday. I don't want to linger here."

Einarr nodded in agreement, then whistled for two other men— Branulf and a thin, wild-haired man named Faralder. Aiden had avoided looking at Faralder so far. The man seemed more than a little mad.

"So, what's the little one's name?" Faralder asked as they walked into the forest, Aiden staying close behind Einarr to avoid getting his rope caught on anything. Aiden didn't answer the question, figuring it wasn't directed at him. Einarr just looked back at him expectantly.

"Does he not speak?" Faralder asked when Aiden was stubbornly silent.

"Not to Einarr," Branulf chuckled. "Little imp hates poor, besotted Einarr's guts."

"Who's besotted?" Einarr looked offended. "Besides, it only makes sense he'd hate all of us for burning his house and taking him with us. He'll get over it in time."

"But he hates you special, Einarr," Branulf teased the other man. "On account of how he thought you were friends. I saw you with him during the trading; how he looked at you all doe-eyed. You're still wearing that token of his, aren't you?"

"I bought this." Einarr covered the token protectively. "It was the only honest trade we saw that day. I'm not just going to throw it out."

"Well, if he isn't going to tell me his name, I'm just going to give him one," Faralder interrupted them to continue on his original tangent. "I don't like little unnamed things. 'Rauthi,' perhaps, for the color of his hair. Or 'Lambi.' He was one of those sheep chasers before, wasn't he? Einarr's little 'Brundalambi.'"

Einarr's face flushed with embarrassment at that, and Branulf laughed loudly. Aiden could only guess that the term meant something derogatory. He scowled at the ground, holding his tongue. He'd endured worse names growing up. He just needed to be patient a while longer. The rope had begun to loosen around his wrists, thanks to his persistent, clandestine pulling and twisting. If he could get it off while they were out here in the woods like this, he could definitely get away.

The three men soon stopped when they located a few fruit trees, pausing to fill their bags. Einarr worked steadily, his progress taking them a little ways from the other two.

"Go on." Einarr nudged Aiden toward one of the trees. "You can reach the low-hanging fruit while I get the higher."

Aiden considered refusing. Why should he do their work for them? But he didn't want to upset them or risk getting sent back to the boat when he was so close to escaping. Einarr stood behind him, close enough for Aiden to feel the warmth of the other man against his back, as they plucked plums from the low branches of the young fruit tree.

"Do you really hate me?"

The question caught Aiden off guard and he looked at Einarr in surprise for a moment before looking stubbornly away, refusing to answer.

"I understand your anger." Einarr spoke softly, sounding almost hurt, "But I had hoped you would understand that I did all I could for you. Branulf would have killed you for challenging him if I hadn't claimed you. Would you hate me for saving your life? What else could I do?"

"You could have not attacked my home!" Anger boiled up in Aiden at Einarr's ignorance and exploded out of him before he could stop himself. "You could have never come to town to begin with! You could have landed on any other beach in the world but mine! You could have done a hundred things that didn't end in everyone I knew dead and me hauled off as a slave! Don't expect me to be happy about that!"

Einarr stared at him, stunned, and a second later, Faralder appeared through the brush, expression concerned.

"Was all that shrieking from him?" the wild-haired man asked, staring at Aiden. "What in the God's name did you do to him?"

"Nothing!" Einarr said sharply. "Go back to your work."

"Were you taking advantage, Einarr?" Faralder teased, seeing that there was no danger. "At least wait until we get home."

"I've told you before, he isn't for that!" Einarr said, more irritated than Aiden had so far seen him.

"Just yell like that again if you need us to come and defend your honor, little Galmr," Faralder said to Aiden with mock seriousness. "Don't worry, I'm sure we'd be able to hear it all the way to the beach."

Einarr threw a plum at Faralder's head and the wild man ran off, giggling madly.

"What does 'Galmr' mean?" Aiden asked as the trees stilled behind him.

"Hmm... Screamer," Einarr replied reluctantly, turning back to the tree. "Try not to let them bother you. Branulf is a brute, and Faralder is half crazy. Their opinions mean nothing. And as for what they keep implying..."

Einarr looked embarrassed, unable to meet Aiden's eye as he focused on a plum he was reaching for.

"That's not my plan for you."

Aiden let that sit in silence for a moment, his anger of a moment before defused somewhat by Faralder's shenanigans, though not remotely dissipated. It was a relief to know he wasn't to become a catamite— a possibility he'd been too terrified to contemplate— but the ominous lack of further explanation left him restless.

"Exactly what is your plan for me?" He gave in at last, asking it flat out.

Einarr took a moment before he replied, thinking over his words carefully, perhaps only now really thinking about what he had taken Aiden for.

"To be honest," he confessed at last. "I don't really have one. I just didn't want you to die. Your bravery in defending that church— it reminded me of my younger brother. And I did not want to bring the gift you carved for my daughter home to her, only to tell her I killed the man who'd made it, though he'd done me no wrong."

Aiden was stumped for a moment, caught off guard by Einarr's reply. He'd expected some ulterior motive, but if Einarr had one, Aiden couldn't sense it in the raw emotion of his response.

"Is your brother among those men?" Aiden asked, curious. "The one I remind you of?"

Einarr paused, reaching for a plum, then shook his head.

"My brother Bard died honorably in battle several years ago." Einarr dropped another plum into his bag, and though he tried to keep his expression distant, his eyes were filled with pain at the memory. "We were all very proud of him. And yet, I would have preferred he died in his bed of old age. I always doted on him too much."

Einarr tried to shrug the story off, hiding his feelings behind his usual smile as he went back to work, but Aiden could see the unhappiness that had settled over him, recalling what had become of Bard. He let things fall back into silence as they continued working.

They cleared the plum trees and moved deeper into the forest. By the time the sun was getting high above them, Faralder had caught a pair of rabbits with his bow, and they'd found fresh water to refill their skins with. The sunlight passed through the transparent leaves like shards of green stained glass and sparkled on the crystal clear water of the spring they'd found. It filled the summer air with its delicate music to the accompaniment of a thousand songbirds, which chattered noisily from every branch. The forest only grew lovelier as the hours passed, and all that time, Aiden had been quietly working at his restraints, getting them loose enough that he thought that he could get them off with one good tug. Now, he just needed to wait for the right moment.

Einarr led them a little away from the others again as they explored, searching for more food to bring back with them. Aiden followed, his heart racing. This was it. If Einarr would just turn his back for a moment, Aiden would be gone.

"Look there," Einarr said, pointing ahead of them to a slim, white tree, its branches heavy with fruit. "Apples. Arnnjorn will be thrilled. They're his favorite."

Together, they began pulling the fruit down from the trees. Aiden eyed Einarr subtly, making sure the man was invested in what he was doing before he turned a little and slipped a sturdy branch between the rope and his wrists, pulling down to help him drag the bond up over his hands. He was so close. He just needed a few seconds more. So long as Einarr stayed engrossed in his apples...

He glanced over at the other man again as he felt the rope slowly giving, sliding up over his thumbs, and froze as he saw something sliding among the branches. A green serpent, almost invisible among the leaves, was winding through the fruit toward Einarr's hand, and the man had not seen it. Aiden felt the rope give way, freeing his hands, just as Einarr reached for an apple hanging just below the snake. For just a moment, Aiden considered doing nothing. Now was his chance. While Einarr was distracted by the snake bite, he could run away. But the serpent might be deadly poisonous, and Einarr had, whatever the circumstances, saved Aiden's life. Aiden made his decision before he'd even realized it, throwing himself at Einarr with a shout to push him back away from the tree. Einarr only stumbled back a few feet, but it was enough to knock him clear of the serpent's strike.

It hung from the branch, jaws still open from its failed strike, hissing hatefully. Aiden watched it from his place against Einarr's chest, his heart racing. He could feel Einarr's heart hammering as quickly as his own, beating just under his hand. The snake retreated into the tree with a final warning hiss, and Aiden breathed a sigh of relief. He looked up at Einarr, who stared down at him, and his unbound hands. Aiden paled with the sudden realization of how much trouble he was in. He turned at once to sprint into the trees, but without the advantage of surprise, Einarr was too much faster than he was. Aiden had gone only a few steps before the other man collided with his back, knocking the wind out of him and driving him into the forest floor. Aiden wheezed as Einarr, heavy and solid, lay on him, his chest to Aiden's back— until Aiden, breathless and frustrated, stopped moving.

He became abruptly, embarrassingly aware of how close to him the other man was. He could feel the heat of Einarr's groin against his backside, and the warmth of his breath stirred Aiden's hair and tickled his ear. He felt a blush rising to his cheeks, humiliation mixing with uneasy fear into a nauseous pit in his stomach. Einarr's hand, pressed into his shoulder blade, slid down his arm, and Aiden's heart skipped a beat. He held his breath, panic fluttering like a caged bird against his ribs, until Einarr's hand reached his wrist, pulling it around to pin it to the small of his own back. He caught Aiden's other hand and pulled it back as well, shifting off of the smaller man in the process. He pulled Aiden up out of the dirt and retied his hands to the rope, tying it tighter this time, and shortening the length of rope between Aiden and where it attached to Einarr's belt. Aiden stood, his hair falling before his face and full of leaves, struggling to catch his breath and deny the angry tears that wanted to overwhelm him. As Einarr finished tying Aiden up, he turned the younger man around by his shoulders and brushed the leaves out of his hair.

"Thank you," he said, somewhat belatedly, "for the snake."

"You're welcome." Aiden's voice was rough with withheld tears, and he couldn't look Einarr in the eye. Einarr, unsatisfied, caught Aiden by the chin and lifted his head, wanting to look him in the face.

"You could have escaped," Einarr stared into Aiden's eyes, brow furrowed with a kind of confused admiration. "You chose to save me instead. Thank you."

Aiden bit the inside of his cheek and looked stubbornly away, still fighting not to cry at the loss of his chance to get away.

"I'm going to start yelling for Faralder," he threatened, and Einarr laughed softly, ruffling Aiden's hair. His hand lingered there longer than usual before he turned away, retrieving his and Aiden's full bags of fruit and game.

"Come along," he said, tugging on the rope. "We've got enough here for the trip home and then some."

They met back up with Branulf and Faralder a little later. Branulf had caught a few decently-sized fish in the stream leading from the spring, and Faralder had found a beehive. He was covered in stings, his beard sticky with honey, and chewing gleefully on a comb when they found him. Together, they headed back to the beach, where Arnnjorn was quite impressed with all they'd found, and mentioned they should mark this place for a camp in the future. Then, they climbed back into the boats to keep going for the rest of the day, though some of the men complained they ought to stay on that shore overnight.

As soon as they were out of sight of the beach, Einarr untied Aiden's hands, frowning at the wounds

Aiden had opened on his wrists from pulling at the rope.

"Are you sure that's wise, Einarr?" Arnnjorn asked as Einarr rinsed Aiden's wrists with water and looked for something to wrap them with. "Your prize might pitch himself overboard."

"He won't go anywhere," Einarr assured Arnnjorn, looking into Aiden's eyes intently. "Will you?"

Aiden thought about it for a moment, then finally shook his head. He wasn't dumb enough to try and swim for it. And regardless, Einarr was right. Aiden had given up. He wasn't getting out of this.

"Besides, he deserves a reward," Einarr said a little louder. "He saved me from a snake today. Little imp slipped his rope and, instead of running, he fought a serpent for me."

Several of the men looked impressed, and Faralder laughed.

"Not just pretty and loud," Faralder grinned at Aiden in amusement. "But crazy as well! That's quite a thrall you've taken, friend."

The mad Viking dabbed some of the honey from his beard and reached over to smear it on Aiden's wrists, making him wrinkle his nose in dismay.

"Honey is good for infection, Gansi," Faralder declared sagely, licking his fingers.

"I'm going to take a wild guess and assume Gansi means 'crazy,'" Aiden asked, deadpan.

"No, that'd be Galinn." Faralder gave a hoot of laughter. "Gansi means 'idiot.'"

Aiden reconsidered throwing himself overboard.

Chapter Four

They sailed until nightfall across open sea. Aiden, relieved to be unbound, but sensing the tenuousness of his position, stayed close to Einarr and tried not to get in the way. There was no moon that night, but the sky was cloudless and the stars were bright, a vast blanket of piercing white light that the ocean reflected so perfectly, it was difficult to tell where one ended and the other began. It was a beautiful sight, but a lonely one which raised in Aiden fears of being lost forever in all that infinite blackness. Einarr was looking out at the stars as well, but from the smile on his face, Aiden couldn't tell if the emptiness bothered him. He was swiftly learning that Einarr used that smile to hide a great deal of what he was feeling.

They didn't make any stops along the coast the next day, and by the time the sun was beginning to get low in the sky, the men were growing restless and talking excitedly to one another of home. Aiden's anxiousness returned as they approached the village, and Einarr retied the rope around his hands, although it was loose and seemed to be a formality more than anything else. Soon, the village was visible, and Aiden was surprised at how similar it looked to his own. Low wood and thatch buildings sprawled across the rock coast near the rough docks. All the houses had a decent amount of space between them, with pens where goats or pigs were kept. A large, long building sat at the center of the town, and it was here that the men hurried as soon as the ships landed, carrying their bounty of silver, lumber, and other goods they'd taken from the English coast.

Aiden followed, pulled along by his rope, as Einarr led him onto the docks and after the others into the hall. The hall was lined with benches, with a fire place in the center. As soon as the men flooded the room, the villagers— the women and children and men too old to go out— came streaming in to join them, bringing with them food and drink in what seemed to Aiden to be positively absurd amounts. Arnnjorn took a seat in a huge chair draped in a bearskin at the end of the hall. The men piled up all the things they'd brought back with them around Arnnjorn's feet, and Einarr brought Aiden there as well, tying him up beside the fire like an animal. Aiden scowled at this indignity, but Einarr just patted him on the head.

"Sit here and behave, and I'll bring you some mead later," he promised and started to turn away, then paused and turned back with a frown and added, "If anyone tries to touch you, bite them and yell."

"Is that something I need to be worried about?" Aiden asked, voice a bit strained.

"Probably not," Einarr reassured him. "But there will be a lot of drinking tonight, so... Just yell loud, alright?"

He hurried off before Aiden could protest any further, and Aiden, irritated, began pulling at the ropes around his hands at once. He'd stay here, but he wasn't going to be hitched to a post like someone's horse, and if Einarr complained, Aiden would just take the man's own advice and bite him.

The celebration was soon in full swing. The huge hall, decorated in furs and tapestries and elaborate carvings, was soon warm and glowing with talk and laughter. The people switched fluidly between the language he'd grown up speaking, which was common in the islands, and a blunt, rolling language, which Aiden didn't know and assumed to be their native tongue. He wondered why they used both so easily if only one was theirs. He also noted that, though they were home and among friends, they kept their weapons always at hand.

He'd just pulled the ropes free when Arnnjorn stood and a hush fell over the assembled men. He began to speak in their native tongue, sweeping his arms to indicate the bounty around him. Aiden watched as he called each of the other men to stand and speak, then divided some portion of the silver and goods to them. For a moment, he was worried he might be included in what was being divided, but the chieftain's hand never pointed in his direction. Then, Faralder stood and said his piece. Arnnjorn assigned him his portion, but instead of sitting down, Faralder, grinning like he was up to some mischief, pointed at Aiden.

Aiden's heart raced with worry, and he searched the room for Einarr, finally finding him at his seat, frowning at Faralder in concern. Faralder wove some story with grand, overwrought gestures, pointing repeatedly to Aiden. When Aiden dared glance at

Einarr again, he saw the man's face was scarlet and he was hiding his mouth behind a hand, clearly boiling with embarrassment. By the time Faralder finished his story, the entire hall was in an uproar of laughter, including Arnnjorn who looked close to weeping with mirth. Finally, he waved a hand at the man dismissively, allowing whatever Faralder had been after. Aiden's chest tightened with distress as the crazy man leapt out of his seat and swept toward him. He looked at Einarr pleadingly, but Einarr was still hiding his face. Within a few long strides, Faralder was standing in front of Aiden proudly. Aiden, kneeling beside the fireplace, looked up at him with wide eyes as Faralder plucked a small piece of silver from the pile of goods. Then, he tossed it into Aiden's hands and, still grinning his mad grin, returned to his seat.

"Your portion of the bounty, thrall," Arnnjorn said in Aiden's language. "For your bravery in defending your home, and in defending Einarr from—"

Here, he paused to glance at Faralder from the corner of his eyes and switched to a decidedly disbelieving tone.

"From the jaws of Jormungander, the Midgard Serpent himself. Truly a heroic act for such a skinny irski."

Faralder tittered like a misbehaving child and nearly fell off his bench.

Aiden stared at the piece of silver in his hand, utterly uncertain how to deal with this.

"All that was won has been divided fairly," Arnnjorn declared a moment later, "Food, silver, cloth, lumber, and one redheaded thrall, who appears to have escaped his ropes again. You are going to have your hands full with this one, I think, Einarr. Are there any who would dispute the fairness of the portions?"

Suddenly, the doors at the end of the hall opened with a rush of chilly night air. Three men, led by a fourth, tall and proud with golden hair, marched into the hall.

"I might dispute it," the man called, striding through the hall to meet Arnnjorn, who stood quickly from his seat.

"Hallvaror Bjornson," Arnnjorn replied, his tone cautiously diplomatic, "you are always welcome in my hall, but if you had sent word ahead, I would have prepared a place for you."

"No place is necessary," Hallvaror declared. "Only what is owed to my father, Jarl Bjorn. Part of this raid is his."

"No man under Bjorn's banner sailed out with us." Arnnjorn's gaze was chilly. "He has no claim to its spoils."

"It was sailed in his ships," Hallvaror argued, "and fought with his weapons."

"Fairly bought and paid for," Arnnjorn replied in an ursine bellow, diplomatic tone forgotten, "and no longer his. I have great respect for the Jarl, but this village is not his, and will not be while I live. He may claim every other quarter of this coast, but we have always stood on our own. If he means to change this, I invite him to come and speak to me as a man about it, not send his son out, demanding what is not his."

"Three times, I have come for the portion that rightfully belongs to the Jarl of this land," Hallvaror spoke just as loudly, with the air of an actor before an audience, proclaiming a mighty speech. "And three times, you have denied him. When winter falls, I shouldn't wonder if the Jarl's sword should fall as well. Fall against you and yours for this insolence."

"This hall has never answered to any King or Jarl!"

"Neither did any of those other settlements up the coast, until they bent the knee to Bjorn, who defends and provides for them. Bjorn the Builder, who creates walls to defend you, and roads to guide you, and great cities to trade from. Only a fool would refuse such a gift."

"Then I am a proud fool," Arnnjorn replied, standing tall and bold. "And will remain so."

Hallvaror's eyes flashed with annoyance, and he glanced at the bounty around them, his eyes lighting on Aiden, who drew back against the fireplace in reflexive fear. A second later, irritated by his own weakness, he froze his expression into one of stony stubbornness, daring anyone to point out that he was shaking.

"Arnnjorn, see reason," Hallvaror said. "Give us some small thing, some token to show my father that you are willing to cooperate, and he may have patience with you. We do not need to waste ourselves on a pointless battle. Send that slave back with me. Surely you won't miss such a thing."

"The thrall is spoken for already," Arnnjorn replied coldly. "He is my nephew Einarr's pledged bounty. And even if he were not, you would not have him. You will leave my hall and you will take nothing with you but what you carried in. Tell your father I will make no deal."

Hallvaror grit his teeth and looked close to reaching for his weapon, but at last, he turned and stormed out of the hall.

"I'll see you again come winter, Arnnjorn," Hallvaror called as he passed through the doors.

The door slammed behind him, and Arnnjorn sat, watching the doors with icy eyes.

The party resumed, now far more subdued, and what Aiden could understand of the conversation was all about what had just happened. Einarr stood and came to Aiden, frowning when Aiden handed him the rope that had previously bound his hands.

"I'm not going to be tied up like a dog," he declared bluntly.

Einarr sighed and shook his head.

"We'll talk about it later," he said as he led Aiden by the shoulder away from the fire. "My family is waiting for us."

"Will we talk about what just happened later, as well?" Aiden asked. "I get the feeling I've been brought here at a very dangerous time."

"That's not far from the truth," Einarr agreed, but he said nothing more as he showed Aiden out of the long house. Aiden noticed a handful of men also leaving, filtering away to the town's houses. Most of them were Einarr's age or older— none were young. Einarr noticed him looking and explained.

"The unmarried men and others with no family live in the hall," he said. "A man doesn't need a house of his own until he has a family. But in Arnnstead, they do not move far from the hall when they marry. We all keep our homes close to the hall and share the livestock, the fields, and outbuildings. Most villages do not do this, but it is our way."

Einarr showed Aiden down the road, some of which was paved with wood or stone to keep it from becoming too muddy. The houses were small, made of turf with stone foundations and living grass growing across the roof. Einarr's was near the end of the road, still within sight of the hall, but a little ways away from everything else. The only wood visible on the outside of the house was the doorway, which made a triangular arch above the entrance. It was elaborately carved, and Aiden paused to admire the work, running his fingers over the complex, knotted images of bears and eagles.

"My father, Arnnjorn's youngest brother, Falki, carved those," Einarr said proudly, stopping to look as well, gaze soft with fondness. "He had almost your talent for carving."

Aiden looked at Einarr's face curiously, always surprised when he saw unguarded emotion there. It was clear the man had missed his home.

As he opened the door, something stirred from within and a second later, Aiden jumped backwards, bristling, as something small and yellow collided with Einarr's middle.

"Faðir, faðir, faðir!" it was chanting and Einarr laughed, patting its yellow head. Gradually, Aiden realized there was a child under all that hair, practically vibrating with excitement as it chattered at incredibly high speed in the Norse tongue. Einarr scooped the child up, cooing something soothing to it, then turned to Aiden.

"This is my girl, Agna," he said, standing straighter with pride. "My Agni. Isn't she a beauty?"

"I'm sure she is," Aiden said, tilting his head to peer at the child curiously, "somewhere under all that hair."

A woman's voice called from deeper in the house, and Aiden heard Agna's name in the rush of unfamiliar words. A moment later, an attractive, dark-haired woman, the corners of her eyes lined with age, appeared around the corner. Einarr greeted her loudly and went to hug her, leaving Aiden standing in the doorway, watching them. An odd discomfort squirmed within him at the sight of the three of them embracing, and he wasn't sure why.

Einarr spoke to her, gesturing to Aiden, and then turned back to Aiden himself.

"Aiden, this is my brother's widow, Jódís," Einarr explained. "She and her mother live here with me, to look after Agni and the house."

"If we left it to the men, everyone would starve," Jódís said, blunt and plainspoken, though there was humor in her tone. "But you did not tell me you would be bringing back thralls this trip."

"I did not plan to," Einarr defended himself from Jódís's accusing look. "But so it is. So, find a place for him to sleep."

Jódís eyed Aiden with just a touch of wary mistrust, but led them inside. The small house was divided into three rooms. Where they'd entered appeared to be a place for storage, lined with shelves and chests, but through a door was the main room, which took the greater part of the house. There were raised benches along the sides as they had in the hall, but these were lower and deeper and covered in furs and blankets. A pot hung above a fire pit in the center of the room, keeping the house warm despite the cool night. A loom was set up near one of the benches, and an old woman— her white hair bound up under a cloth the same as Jódís— was at work on it, her fingers steady and methodical. Jódís fetched a fur from one of the benches and spread it on the dirt floor next to one of the benches near the fire.

"Dísa, there is space for him," Einarr said, dissatisfied. "There's no need for him to be on the ground."

Jódís looked at him for a moment, obviously confused.

"Einarr, he's a thrall," she said. "The floor is where he belongs. Look, he'll even be at your feet while you sleep."

The old woman raised her head, blinking blindly at the room around her, and mumbled a question containing the word "thrall."

"There's just no point in it when we have the space," Einarr argued, picking up the fur and tossing it back onto one of the benches. "Why make him less comfortable than he needs to be?"

Jódís looked perplexed, but she threw her hands up, disinclined to argue.

"You'll be wanting the goats to have beds as well, next, I shouldn't wonder," she muttered as she moved away, catching Agna out of Einarr's arms and taking her off to sit on one of the benches, where she seemed to have been in the middle of combing out and braiding the girl's hair.

"Don't mind her," Einarr said to Aiden with a smile. "She'll warm up to you in time."

Aiden somehow doubted that. But he was increasingly uncertain of his place here now. Was he a slave, a part of the family, something in-between? He didn't know what to expect anymore.

"So, is she Agna's mother?" he asked, figuring a change of subject was better.

"No, Agna's mother died when she was still a babe," Einarr said with a touch of sadness. "It was a sudden illness. We hadn't been married long. Dísa was Bard's wife, but they never had children before Bard died fighting."

Aiden regretted his change of subject immediately and looked away, guilt a stone in his stomach. He searched for something else to ask about, but everything felt awkward now. He couldn't decide how to feel. The fear he'd felt during the boat ride had abated into a kind of uneasy resignation, just waiting for what would happen next, leaving the way open to mourn the home and people he'd lost. They may not have liked him, but they were still all he'd ever known. Now, he was caught between anxiety and tired misery. The uncertainty was beginning to make him nauseous. These quaint domestic scenes didn't match with the violence he was still half-expecting. He was beginning to gather that Einarr was not treating him as a normal thrall. His worries about becoming the older man's bedfellow returned briefly and distressingly, and he tried to dismiss them as entirely too upsetting to consider for the moment. Nothing was clear, and Aiden wasn't certain if he wanted to cry, run, fight, or just go to bed. He felt exhausted by the emotions that were pulling him in so many directions.

Einarr asked Jódís to bring some food for Aiden since he hadn't been able to eat at the celebration. He sat on his bench and, at a dagger-like stare from Jódís, Aiden sat on the floor at Einarr's feet and accepted the bread and fruit Einarr handed him. He tried not to let being made to sit on the floor bother him, but it nagged at him. Jódís, and probably Einarr, and certainly the other men, didn't consider him a person. Or at least not as much of a person as they were. He was something closer to an animal in their eyes. Nothing more than a particularly intelligent dog. It was not a good feeling. Was that his place now? Einarr's weird, spoiled pet?

Einarr and Jódís talked after Jódís finished Agna's hair and put her to bed, but it was in indecipherable Norse. Aiden could only sit in silence on the floor, feeling more like furniture than a person, until a little later, Einarr shooed him off to his bench.

"Rest well tonight," Einarr said as Aiden climbed into the box-like bed and fussed with his blankets. "We'll have a lot to do tomorrow."

Aiden hummed his wordless agreement and rolled to face the wall as Einarr doused the lanterns, his worries sinking onto him like a heavy weight that crushed the breath from his lungs. Einarr hadn't bothered to tie him up again. When they were asleep, Aiden could easily just get up and leave. And go where? He was an ocean away from everything familiar to him. He had nothing, save the small piece of silver Faralder had bestowed on him. He wasn't certain about the value of silver, but he didn't think it would get him far. Most likely, it was just enough to make him worth robbing. He reached into his pocket to touch it, and found something smooth instead. He pulled it out, frowning as he realized it was the blue bead Einarr had traded to him. He was struck briefly with the desire to throw it, but he didn't. He eyed it by the light of the dying fire a little longer, and then tucked it back into his pocket again, resigning himself to his new life. It hadn't come in the way he would have hoped, but he had wished for change. And at least he wasn't alone anymore. Sort of.

Chapter Five

The next morning, he woke early to the sound of Jódís returning to the house from some early morning chore. She was carrying a bucket of water and poured part of it into a basin near the fire, which was just embers now. The rest of the house was stirring now, grumbling softly as they rose. Agna whined and tried to go back to sleep, but when Jódís pushed food into her hands, she sat up to eat. Jódís gave food to everyone, even, reluctantly, to Aiden. Einarr put his food aside at first and instead went to the basin to splash water on his face and hands and his long, golden hair. Aiden watched curiously as Einarr brushed out his damp hair and beard with a long comb made of bone. Then, he carried to basin to the door to empty it and refilled it from the bucket before passing it to Jódís's mother, who did the same and passed it to Jódís, who washed herself and Agna. While they cleaned, Einarr ate and cleaned his nails with a little metal pick. When they finished, he waved to Aiden.

"Come here," he said. "We'll begin to get that English stink off of you today."

Aiden frowned, offended, but he had to admit, all of the people he'd met here were far cleaner and nicer-smelling than those he'd grown up with. He supposed doing this every day must contribute, though it seemed like such a waste of time. Still, he went to Einarr's side and, when the man gestured for Aiden to sit at his feet, Aiden scowled, but complied.

"Here, clean your face and hands." Einarr pushed the basin toward him. "You still have dirt on your cheek from where I tackled you in the woods after the snake."

When Aiden hesitated, Einarr plunged his hands into the basin and splashed water on Aiden's face himself, ignoring Aiden's startled sputtering as he scrubbed the dirt away. He poured more water into Aiden's hair, making him gasp at the coldness, and then began combing his red curls out with quick, efficient strokes that tugged painfully at Aiden's scalp. He grimaced, but held still, too confused to resist.

"Really, Einarr?" Jódís looked at her brother combing Aiden's hair and shook her head in disgust. "It's indecent."

"Do you want him to go on smelling like a sheep?" Einarr asked pointedly. "I'm teaching him how to do it."

Jódís scoffed and picked up Agna, hiding her eyes as she carried the girl outside.

"You'll get a proper bath on Saturday," Einarr promised, unbothered by his sister-in-law's opinions. "But this should help for now."

"Help with what?" Aiden grumbled, wincing as Einarr pulled on a knot. "You'll make me bald."

"Clean hair and skin makes a man healthier and handsomer," Einarr pronounced, tearing out another tangle.

Once the worst of the tangles were gone, the combing actually became rather soothing. Aiden thought he could get used to the gentle scrape of the teeth over his scalp, and the way Einarr's fingers felt sliding through his hair after it. He leaned back against the other man's leg without thinking, relaxing into the surprisingly intimate contact. A touch grazed the shell of his ear and he shivered, suddenly remembering where he was. He pulled away, flustered.

"I think that's enough," he said, patting at his hair, which was weirdly soft now. "Anymore and I really will go bald."

"Suit yourself," Einarr chuckled. "Sit there; I'll find you something clean to wear."

He stood and went to the storage room while Aiden looked down at the clothes he'd worn and slept in since he'd inherited them from his father. He'd never had any other clothes besides them before. Was something else really necessary?

A minute later, Einarr had forced him into a tunic the color of summer flowers, rich blue with embroidery at the collar and hemmed in red thread.

"Father Maredudd would not approve of this vanity," Aiden said, holding the bottom out to examine the embroidery.

"It was Bard's when he was a boy." Einarr scooped up Aiden's old clothing, wrinkling his nose at the stench and tossing it into a little pit in the corner out of the way. "You're so small! I was worried I'd have to give you something of Agni's."

It was a little big on him, Aiden thought, tugging self-consciously at the collar, which kept slipping toward his shoulder.

Once Aiden was dressed, they stepped outside where Jódís and Agna were feeding the goats with the women from the next house over. Jódís stared at Aiden in surprise as he came out.

"Well," she said, "he is a lovely thing once he's cleaned up, isn't he? I was hardly expecting there to be a human being under all that dirt."

She handed the rest of the feed to Agna and left the pen as the other women crowded to the edge of the enclosure to look at Aiden as well.

"Did you really fight a giant snake for Einarr?" one of them asked.

"Jormungander himself, I heard," the other teased.

"I'm going to strangle Faralder," Einarr said, face red. "It was an adder, and a sizable one, but it was no Midgard serpent. Still, it likely would have bitten me if Aiden hadn't spotted it first. I owe him a debt."

Einarr ruffled Aiden's still-drying curls and Aiden looked away, hunching his shoulders in embarrassment.

"So, what are we doing?"

After Einarr had talked with Jódís and Agna a little longer, he turned and led Aiden away, and Aiden hurried to keep up, wondering where they were heading.

"It's time for the summer harvest," Einarr explained. "We do the planting in spring, before we go out to raid, and come back in time to gather it in. In the larger settlements, they have a second raid once the harvest is done, but we do not have the numbers for this. And no one wants to be abroad during winter."

The fields were not far from the village's cluster of houses and were not separated by who owned them. The entire town worked a single, massive field and, Einarr explained, Arnnjorn divided up the harvest fairly according to needs and deeds. The largest families received the most, followed by those who had earned the greatest honors during the raids. Any man could challenge Arnnjorn if they thought the distribution was unfair, and he would hear their argument. It was a very different system from what Aiden was accustomed to. He could hardly imagine working such a huge field just to hand it over to someone else and hope they gave you back enough to live on. But he supposed it seemed to be working for Arnnstead. He'd hardly seen anyone who looked starving or sickly since he'd arrived.

The morning sun was still faint, its light a weak, watery blue as they approached the field. Mist spread its milky fingers between the high, golden stalks of barley and rye and hid entirely the green vegetables growing in the lower fields, making pools and ponds of swirling, pearly fog. Insects sang their rattling songs in the grasses, and the first birds were beginning to answer those calls with musical trills of their own; quiet voices murmured behind the repetitive, metallic rush of sickles and scythes cutting through the grain. A cool morning breeze stirred the shoulder-high sea of gold with silver waves and tugged at Aiden's hair, and he thought he'd never seen so much food— so much wealth— in one place. He breathed in deeply, the scent of damp earth in his nose, and felt, for a moment, more optimistic about his new life.

"Einarr, who's this?"

Faralder came loping out of the field, dropping his sickle as he approached them. Branulf ambled after him, slower and without carelessly discarding his tools. Faralder grabbed Aiden by the face, making him flinch and squirm to try and get away.

"Is this the grubby little snake charmer you brought back with you?" Faralder teased. "I hardly recognize him! Just look at that hair! He's like a burning torch!"

"Am I still allowed to bite people?" Aiden asked Einarr, eyeing Faralder's hand.

"You're allowed to bite Faralder."

Faralder quickly pulled his hands away.

"And stop telling that story," Einarr scolded. "It was embarrassing enough the first time."

Faralder grinned, but Branulf was frowning at Aiden seriously.

"Is that thrall wearing Bard's tunic?" he asked seriously. "And you still haven't put a collar on him."

"The tunic is old and was going to waste," Einarr said dismissively, "and I'll get to the collar. I haven't had time yet."

"Einarr," Branulf's voice was deadly serious, "taking a thrall for your bed is one thing. You've been wed and had children. No one's going to object to you enjoying yourself now. But letting a thrall wander around unbound and in your brother's clothes... You're heading in a dangerous direction, friend."

"What's dangerous?" Faralder scoffed. "He's harmless! Just look at the little dandelion."

He patted Aiden's now dry and admittedly somewhat wild hair. Aiden considered making good on his threat to bite the man, but thought that might undermine his argument. And while he wasn't certain how thralls were supposed to be treated, he had a feeling he preferred Einarr's method.

"Let Einarr go a little eccentric in his old age, will you?" Faralder pleaded.

"I'm not old," Einarr grumbled. "I'm only thirty."

Branulf sighed and threw his hands in the air.

"Let's just get back to work, shall we?" he said, and together they moved into the field.

The work was exhausting and tedious. Aiden's arms were burning, and his hands were beginning to blister from holding up his sickle before even a few hours had passed. The men worked in lines to take down the wheat. The women followed behind to pick it up and bind it so it could dry before threshing. Despite how back-breaking it was, Einarr and the others almost seemed to be enjoying it. They bantered back and forth as they went, trading playful insults and sharing gossip. Aiden finally learned why they flowed so easily from one language to the next. It seemed the men took brides from the islands as often as they did from home. A good half of the men's mothers had all been from the English coast, and they'd been raised speaking their mother's tongue as easily as their father's. Maredudd would have had a fit, Aiden thought. And that was before he learned that marriage here was not as straightforward as he was used to.

Men were known to take more than one wife, or a wife and several concubines. And on some occasions, women took more than one husband. It seemed dishonesty was a greater offense to them than adultery. To sleep with another was fine. To sleep with another and not tell your spouse about it was grounds for divorce. His head was spinning as much from what he was learning as from exhaustion by the time they stopped for lunch when the sun was directly above them and beating down hard on their heads. Aiden fell into the grass feeling like a cut string, limp and liquid, and Einarr and the others joined him shortly while one of the women handed out food for everyone. As she leaned over to hand Einarr his meal, Aiden noticed the iron collar glinting dully at her throat. He swallowed hard at the sight of it, and upon looking closer, he noticed that her clothes were more plain and worn than the other women's as well. She must be another thrall. She ignored him, passing him over without giving him any food, until Einarr called her back and made her serve him as well. Aiden couldn't mistake the look of bitter, envious anger she gave him as she dropped the food in his lap and moved on. Guilt and embarrassment ate at him. Glancing around, he spotted more iron collars, some still working the field despite the sun. Others sat in a group not far from him, eating thin, cold fish instead of the bread and fruit Aiden and the free men had been given. Aiden's guilt worsened.

"Here, try this," Einarr said, offering Aiden a bowl of something white and creamy. "It's skyr. You'll love it."

Aiden could see Branulf observing disapprovingly, and he was painfully aware of the men behind him with their meager, unappealing lunch.

"That's alright." Aiden looked away, holding up a hand to ward Einarr off. "I'm fine with this."

Einarr looked disappointed briefly, but went back to eating without pressing the issue. Aiden nibbled at his own food, guilt turning his stomach sour.

By that evening, a good portion of the field had been harvested, and the men returned to the long house for dinner. Again, Einarr had Aiden sit with him and the other men and fed him meat and cheese while, across the hall, the other thralls sat on the floor at their masters' feet and ate their own meager meals. Even the sweet, honeyed mead Einarr insisted Aiden try could do nothing to improve Aiden's mood. His feelings swung between gratitude that he was being spared the life of a proper thrall, fear that Einarr would tire of him and that would become his life, and gut-wrenching shame that he should be sitting here drinking mead and wearing no collar while they had to watch. He could feel the intense dislike in their gazes whenever they looked at him, and he knew it was entirely justified. Other free men had begun giving him strange looks as well, clearly not approving of how Einarr was spoiling him. He began to reconsider running away.

They left the hall late, well-fed and, in Einarr's case, warmed by several horns of mead. They took their time walking back, Einarr pausing to enjoy the cool night air and the blue-black sky full of brilliant stars. A pale sliver of moon was set in the brow of the night like a silver diadem, the stars glimmering diamonds radiating around it. Einarr stopped to look out over the dark ocean as it rolled gently against the docks, the creaking of the boats and the soothing rush of surf almost erasing the laughter and music from the hall behind them. Aiden wished he could enjoy it more, but his feelings were still too conflicted.

"Einarr," he started as he looked up at the other man, biting the inside of his cheek with worry.

"That's the first time you've said my name," Einarr, surprised and pleased, looked away from the horizon back to the other man with a smile. "Does that mean you're starting to like me?"

"What's a thrall?"

Einarr looked taken aback by the question, his smile falling.

"That's what I am, aren't I?" Aiden pressed on, "But you don't treat me the way the other thralls are treated. And we don't have them where I'm from, so maybe I just don't understand. So, explain it to me. What am I, Einarr?"

Einarr was quiet for a long moment, considering his answer.

"They say the God Ríg created the race of thralls first." Einarr looked away back over the ocean again, clearly feeling uncomfortable. "Then the bondi, the freemen, and the jarls, the nobility. And one was always meant to serve the other. To be a thrall is to be born with a destiny of servitude. It's a fate they can change, if they work for it. A thrall can buy his freedom for eight ounces of silver. But until then, they are..."

He paused, obviously unsure how to say what he needed to in a tactful way.

"Less than human," he finished at last, and Aiden felt the words like a stab.

"Am I less than human, Einarr?" Aiden asked, his hands clenched in his tunic.

"You're a thrall." Einarr shifted uneasily, unable to answer the question directly. "You're clever and lovely, but you're a thrall. Born without freedom."

"Except I wasn't," Aiden said, anger mixing with his hurt. "I was free as any man before you came along. *You* chose this life for me, not fate or destiny. Did you want me for a pet? Something cute and subhuman you could let sit at your feet and admire? Is that all I am in your eyes?"

"No!" Einarr's reply was loud, shocking Aiden, who flinched away. Einarr, looking guilty, tried again more gently.

"No, Aiden." He reached out for the smaller man carefully. "The first time you smiled at me, all I could think was that I wanted to see more. And when I thought Branulf was going to kill you, my heart broke at the thought of never seeing that smile again. So, I stopped him the only way I knew how. I don't regret raiding your town. I can't, because it's allowed me to keep you here with me, and it's given me hope that I might see you smile at me again. I had to make you a thrall to keep you, but I can't bear to make you unhappy."

Aiden's heart was racing as Einarr's hands, flushed with warmth from too much drink, brushed his hair back from his cheek and held his face, delicately as if he were cupping a fragile flower. His feelings once again eluded him— the bright flicker of strange happiness he felt at hearing Einarr's feelings was at war with his fear and his anger and his guilt. His feelings for Einarr were as tumultuous as the sea in a storm. The man had been nothing but kind to him, but had equally been at least partially responsible for the destruction of Aiden's home. He'd saved Aiden's life, at the cost of making him a slave. And then there was the way he was looking at Aiden right now, intense and heated, making Aiden's heart flutter in a way he didn't understand. He was afraid, and yet there was no part of him that wanted to run away from Einarr.

And then, Einarr bent and pressed his lips to Aiden's. Aiden's heart leapt into his throat. Einarr smelled of warm leather and tasted of mead. His hands were firm and commanding at the small of Aiden's back as Einarr pressed him closer. Aiden could feel the rough scratch of the other's man's beard against his skin. His hands splayed on Einarr's chest; he could feel the man's heart beating almost as frantically as his own. For a moment, he was too stunned to think— he could only feel. The way his skin warmed at Einarr's touch, the way his lips tingled at every brush of the other man's mouth against them, the electric current that seemed to run up his spine. But then, almost at once, every sermon Maredudd had ever given came back to him. Maredudd had spoken only rarely on the abomination of man lying with man. The father found the topic distasteful. But whenever he had brought it up, he had addressed it with only the most vitriolic hate and disgust. It was sin as loathsome as bestiality or the rape of children in his eyes and, according to him, in God's eyes. Any sex that wasted a man's seed with no chance of bearing children was equally abhorrent. And especially abhorrent was the man who let himself be used as a woman.

Aiden pushed away, panicking as sudden shame and fear overwhelmed him. For a moment, Einarr's arms stayed locked around him, and he was afraid the other man wouldn't let him go, but a moment later, he had struggled free, stumbling back a few steps, out of the range of Einarr's arms. Einarr stared after him, at first confused, then hurt, then guilty, emotions flitting across his handsome features like shadows across the moon.

"I'm sorry," he spoke as gently as he could, taking another step back. "I shouldn't have... You know I never intended to use you that way."

"It's fine," Aiden said quickly, shoulders hunched, refusing to look the other man in the eye. "You just had too much to drink. You should go to bed."

Einarr looked close to arguing for a moment, but then, he nodded in agreement and turned away. Aiden followed a few steps behind, his body fairly vibrating with anxious emotion. When they reached home, Jódís and Agna were, mercifully, already asleep. Aiden went straight to his bed and Einarr, with a few last shameful glances in Aiden's direction, went to his own.

Aiden lay sleepless for a long while, despite how exhausted he was from the day's work. He pressed his fingers to his lips, tingling like the ghost of Einarr's mouth was still there. He closed his eyes, remembering for a moment what it had felt like to be held that way. The warmth of Einarr's kiss, the strength of his arms. His body ached, from more than just working, and he quickly pulled his hands away from his mouth.

He'd been so afraid of it happening against his will— of being made into an object for someone else's enjoyment. But how much worse would it be, in the eyes of the God he'd been baptized to and raised in the name of, if he went to it willingly?

Chapter Six

The next morning, they ate and washed as they had yesterday. Aiden went last, and Einarr made no offer to comb his hair for him today; in fact, Einarr said little to him at all until they were about to leave. He stopped Aiden at the door, turned him back around, and held something out to him. Aiden felt a cold pit grow in his stomach as he saw it was a rough iron collar, thin and plain. Aiden's shoulders slumped tiredly.

"I could give you all the reasons," Einarr said, "but you know why."

Aiden nodded, solemn and resigned, and tilted his head back, offering his neck to Einarr. This was life now. He'd do what he needed to in order to keep living it.

Einarr slid the cold metal around his throat, but it was the brush of his warm fingers that made Aiden shiver and then bite his tongue in shame. The lock was a simple hook and eye. Aiden heard it click into place, and then Einarr turned him around, gently brushed the hair away from the back of his neck, and with a pair of pliers, bent the hook so that it would no longer fit through the eye. At least not without help. His fingers grazed the nape of Aiden's neck, just below where the collar sat, lingering there just a moment too long.

Aiden stepped away and reached up to touch the iron band, then took a deep breath. It was loose enough that it didn't press against his skin or make breathing difficult, but it was heavy enough that he could feel it every time he moved or drew breath— a constant reminder that he wasn't a person. His only choices now were between pet dog and work horse. The worst part seemed to be that he wouldn't be able to hide it. Everyone would see what he was now.

For the next two days, they tiptoed around each other, hoping they could find some equilibrium to settle into. Einarr seemed to be trying to give Aiden his space. When they did have to interact for one reason or another, he treated Aiden like something impossibly delicate and fragile, speaking to him only in hushed tones, touching him only with the most hesitant care. Frustration simmered below the surface of Aiden's every action, growing closer to a boil every time Einarr looked at him with that faraway longing in his eyes.

"Do you think we'll go to war with Jarl Bjorn?"

They were at work in the fields, the end of the harvest finally in sight. Some of the stalks were dry enough for the threshing to have begun, but most of the men were still focused on clearing the field. Aiden worked near Einarr, Faralder, and Branulf as he always did. Branulf posed the question so casually, he might as well have been inquiring about the weather.

"It seems likely," Einarr agreed. "Arnnjorn has no intention of bending the knee to him. I have to admit, I also don't care for the idea of being under the Jarl's banner. We've always done things our own way here, and it's a way I like."

"I feel the same," Branulf agreed. "But it's not a war we'll win; I can tell you that. Bjorn's army is too large. I shouldn't be surprised if he outnumbers us twenty to one."

"Better to die fighting than go willingly," Faralder chimed in. "I won't be beholden to some king I've never seen."

Branulf nodded solemnly in agreement, his sickle moving methodically through the barley.

"Arnnjorn is the man I know, the man I've followed into battle a hundred times or more, and it's him I'll follow again. Not an unproven jarl. And certainly not his smug worm of a son."

Einarr was not so quick to agree, frowning and pausing in swinging his sickle.

"To die in battle is a fine thing," he said after a moment. "But there are things here I want to keep alive. Agna, Jódís."

He glanced in Aiden's direction, but left the statement unfinished.

"Perhaps it would be better to die in another battle." He resumed his work, focusing hard on the stalks to avoid looking at Aiden again. "One that the lives of our home and families don't depend on."

"So, you're saying you'd rather we roll over and let Bjorn have us?" Branulf asked scornfully.

"If it's a choice between that and destruction," Einarr tried to explain, "Wouldn't it be better to meet Bjorn halfway? I have heard no tales of horror from the towns he's made himself king of. Indignation about the portion he takes of their harvests and bounties. But he has let no one starve yet."

"And what about when he dies?" Faralder pointed out, "And that awful son of his becomes Jarl? Do you think Hallvaror will be so generous?"

"A man like that sees a chance to take something, he takes it all." Branulf paused, leaning on his scythe. "With no consideration for the season to come. He is too unwise."

"Then we'll deal with Hallvaror when he becomes a problem," Einarr argued, stopping as well. "We won't live to see what kind of Jarl he becomes if we resist his father now."

Faralder sighed.

"It's not in any of our hands, anyway," he said, picking up his sickle again. "And all arguing about it is doing is slowing down our work. Bjorn is a worry for winter. Now, who thinks they can beat me to the end of this row?"

Seizing on the distraction, the three men hurried off, working as fast as they could. Aiden stayed behind, working at his steady pace, but their words lingered worryingly in his mind. It seemed like a bad time to live in Arnnstead. A sudden memory of the night his home had burned hit him like a brick. Images of fire and death leapt before his eyes. His sickle slipped and nearly caught him in his leg. He dropped it, but when he crouched to retrieve it, found he couldn't get back up. Panic had settled like a weight in his chest, filling him with dread at the thought of that chaos happening again— happening here. The faces in the church that looked up at him were Agna and Jódís. It was Einarr lying dead in the road, and the image sent a stab of genuine pain through his chest. He couldn't breathe. He clutched at his aching chest, fear drowning him though he was in no danger.

He felt a warm, strong hand on his shoulder, rubbing circles on his back. A familiar voice was speaking in his ear, calling him back from the nightmare he was caught in. He looked up and into Einarr's eyes, which were full of concern and affection. He suddenly wanted to throw himself into the other man's arms and be held, but he didn't dare. Einarr helped him to his feet instead and led him out of the way of the other people working.

"Just sit here till you can breathe again," Einarr was saying. "You're safe. Everyone is here to protect you. There's nothing to be afraid of."

Aiden wished that were true.

Einarr returned to his work and, after a few more minutes, Aiden had calmed down enough to go back to work as well, though panic lingered at the edge of everything for the rest of the day, just waiting to be set off again. He did his best not to think about the future.

The next day was Saturday, and in the morning, Jódís woke everyone early to eat and get ready to go bathe. She piled dirty laundry in his arms and carried the bathing tools as she led her still-yawning family up the hill behind the house. Aiden wasn't sure what to expect, but in the place where several small hills made a hollow, stones had been driven into the ground surrounding a deep pool, steaming in the early morning chill. It was fed by a spring, which fell through the rocks above it, making liquid music through the silence before even the birds were awake. As soon as they reached the pool, Einarr and the others began shedding their clothes, Einarr leaving his ax on the edge in easy reach. Aiden, his arms still full of laundry, lingered, unsure of what to do. Jódís soon answered that question, stepping in front of him as he was trying not to look at Einarr's back.

"Thralls bathe last," she said bluntly. "Take the clothes up the hill. There's a second pool there. Start the washing. I'll come up and finish it when we're done."

Aiden nodded, the collar heavy on his neck as he did as he was told. He glanced back only once at the family bathing, Einarr laughing at Agna splashing in the water. His chest ached with the sudden desire to have a place among them. Equally painful was the acceptance that he never would. The collar made certain of that.

He hadn't been working on the laundry long before other thralls, scrubbing at tired eyes, wandered up the hill to work next to him. Some chatted tiredly with one another, but for the most part, they were silent, the laughter and talk from the larger hot spring below drifting up toward them. After an hour or so, Jódís appeared and took over, telling him to go and wash the sheep stink from his skin at last. Aiden didn't argue, hurrying back down the rocky hill. Bathing had never been a common thing where he'd grown up, but since he'd begun washing every morning, he found he enjoyed being clean and was looking forward to being thoroughly washed.

When he reached the pool, he saw one of the neighbors saying a warm goodbye to Einarr as he climbed out. Einarr remained in the pool, though all his family had clearly finished already. He lay back with his arms on the stone, just soaking and enjoying himself. His hair, clean and golden, sat in wet spirals against his broad shoulders. Moisture glistened on his muscular chest, running over the intricate tattoos that covered his arms and ran up his throat. The heat had brought an attractive glow to his cheeks. Aiden hesitated as he approached, trying not to stare. Should he wait for the other man to finish before he got in? He found himself balking at the thought of undressing in front of Einarr. But as he waffled a few steps away, Einarr spotted him and waved him over.

"Don't worry," he said, "Go ahead and climb in. I'll deal with Jódís if she makes a fuss."

Aiden bit his lip, debating for a moment, but at last, he pulled his tunic off over his head and stepped out of his shoes. He would never be as big as Einarr or Branulf— he was just built lean— but he'd worked hard all his life and was decently strong, with wiry muscle corded beneath his fair, freckled skin. He found himself hesitating again as he reached for his pants, aware of Einarr's eyes on him, but at last, he pushed them off as well, sliding into the hot water across from the older man, trying hard not to look at him.

The water was almost too hot, sinking into his muscles like teeth. He sighed as he settled in and the heat burrowed into him, loosening all the tension he'd built up. For a moment, he forgot Einarr was there altogether in how wonderful it felt. He easily could have fallen asleep against the stones, but he remembered the other man's presence and regathered his senses. He began splashing water over his face and hair, trying to hurry and wash before Jódís came back.

"I've wanted to speak with you alone," Einarr spoke from the other side of the spring, "To apologize for the other day. I should not have done what I did."

It took Aiden a moment to realize he was talking about the kiss, and he shook his head dismissively.

"You were drunk," Aiden shrugged, trying to pretend it had meant nothing. "You probably would have kissed Faralder if he'd been in arm's reach."

"No," Einarr replied with quiet certainty, "I was not so drunk I couldn't tell you from Faralder. And I was not so drunk I would have kissed anyone but you."

Aiden looked away, unable to bear the calm and unshakable affection in Einarr's eyes. He hoped the steam of the pool disguised the flush on his cheeks.

"Still, I should never have done it," Einarr continued, shifting to lean forward. "I know you English do not see such things the same way we do. And it has only been a short time since you were brought here. I would not blame you if you still hated me. I only hope that, one day, you will be able to see me as a friend."

Aiden dared to look at the other man, the sincerity in his eyes searing, his damp, golden hair sticking to his cheek. Aiden's heart ached in his chest.

"I don't hate you."

He said it barely loud enough to be heard, and he couldn't bring himself to say more about the wild wind of emotions that hurled themselves around his insides every time he looked at Einarr. He didn't dare speak of the fearful conflict within him, the dread of hell, the doubt of its existence, versus the way his heart raced at the memory of that kiss. And beside it all, anxiety gripped his heart at the thought of allowing such a thing, of debasing himself that way, only to see Einarr lose interest in him the moment some other, more worthy partner appeared.

Despite his silence, at Aiden's words, Einarr stood, water sliding down the planes of his abdomen as he moved across the spring. The pool was deep in the center, but at the edges was a ring of stones to sit on. As Einarr came to stand in front of Aiden, crossing the deeper center of the pool, Aiden's eyes were level with Einarr's waist. He felt his stomach twisting with nervousness, but he didn't move as Einarr reached down to brush a scarlet curl away from his cheek.

"If you do not despise me," Einarr spoke in a low purr of a voice that seemed to vibrate in Aiden's bones, "Then why not let me show you all I could do for you?"

Aiden wanted to protest, but the words stuck in his throat. He froze, trembling, as Einarr's fingers grazed his jaw. A million reasons to resist or give in clamored for attention in his mind. If he gave in, God would reject him. If he resisted, it might be Einarr who rejected him. He might find himself sold to the next passing trader. Or Einarr might take what he wanted anyway... Unable to decide, he simply did nothing, still as stone as Einarr bent to kiss him, his lips warm and tasting of spring water. His hands slid below the water to caress Aiden's thighs, and an electric shiver ran up his spine. Einarr's tongue pushed past Aiden's lips to ravish his mouth. Aiden felt lightheaded and too warm, feeling like he was almost melting as Einarr's big, rough hands squeezed his hips and ran with surprising delicacy over his stomach, which trembled under his touch. Aiden's indecisive mind still scrambled to justify what was happening in one direction or the other, but his body had already made its choice, leaning into Einarr's kiss, returning it with fevered passion.

Suddenly, they heard men's voices, laughing as they came up the hill toward the pool. Aiden pulled away with a panicked little gasp, and Einarr reluctantly pulled his hands away and sat down beside Aiden, both of them trying to calm their shallow, excited breathing before Faralder and Branulf appeared, leading a host of women and children.

"Einarr!" Faralder laughed. "Are you still bathing at this hour? I thought your family was supposed to go early so you'd be out of the way before everyone else!"

"Privilege of having the house closest to the hill," Einarr called back. "I get to soak as long as I like. You're looking lovely this morning, Hilda!"

He waved to one of the women with Faralder, a plump and dark-haired young lady, who waved back with a bright grin.

"She's pregnant again!" Faralder said proudly, putting his arm around her and a thinner, redheaded woman as well. "Her and Mýrún both!"

Aiden noticed that, of the innumerable pack of children excitedly tearing off their clothing and splashing into the spring, only two didn't bear a striking resemblance to Faralder and his wives.

"Freyr has over-blessed you, friend." Einarr shook his head, laughing. "Half the village will be your children at this rate."

"Perhaps they'll have to start calling it Faraldstead!" Faralder agreed with a laugh, also stripping naked to climb in beside his children and wives. Branulf and his wife and kids were getting in as well. Suddenly feeling crowded, Aiden ducked to quickly wash his hair, then scrambled out when no one was looking and quickly pulled on his clothes. He didn't dare look back to see if Einarr was watching him as he scurried away, hurrying far enough away that he couldn't hear the talk and laughter any longer before he sat to comb out his hair with shaking hands, almost dropping the elk horn comb Einarr's family shared.

Behind the rocky hill, the land sloped up, the hills growing taller and more bare until they became the feet of cliffs and mountains not so far away. It was still early, the sky a pale cornflower blue beyond the slate peaks with their heads of snow, unmelted even in summer. The spears of violet flowers waved in the breeze off the ridge, carrying their scent back up toward Aiden, vibrant against the blanket of green moss and grass that covered the hills in emerald, which crashed like a verdant wave against the stony slopes, capped by crests of jagged boulders.

The view reminded Aiden of home, and of sitting on the moor with his sheep. He missed those quiet hours. He missed carving. He even missed the sheep. Things had been miserable then, but simple. He'd understood his place in the world. He'd known precisely what path his life would take, gray and dismal as that path might have been. Now, looking out over that wild and empty landscape, he had no idea where he belonged, or what would happen to him, or what he should do.

"God," he found himself whispering to those mountains, "If there is a God. You were such a fact of life before that I never thought to doubt you. But you don't live here, and these people are happier and more prosperous than Maredudd's flock ever was. But if you exist, and if I have ever been anything to you, then tell me what I'm meant to do."

Only silence and the breeze off the mountain answered him. Aiden went on waiting, hoping, but felt nothing. His stomach seemed to tangle itself in knots with his frustration.

"Then, if the Northmen's Gods are listening..." His voice cracked as he tried again, "I don't know your names or what you would ever want with me, but if you could send me some sign, any little thing to just show me why I'm here, I would be yours forever. I would learn every word that's known of you and sing it till the day I died. Please. Just show me something."

Once again, there was no reply. A fat, glossy crow flew by, cawing noisily in the still summer air, erupting out of the grass so suddenly, Aiden jumped. He stared after it, startled, but if it was a sign, it wasn't one Aiden understood. He sighed and gave up. He supposed he had no choice but to discover his place on his own.

"Galinn! Little crazy one, is that you there?"

Aiden stood, confused, as he heard Faralder calling to him from down the hill. He moved to the crest of the hill, until he could see the other man, who was now dressed again. Aiden must have been sitting there so long, he and his family had finished washing.

"I'm here!" Aiden replied. "Do you need me?"

"Has Agna gone past you?" Faralder shouted. "Have you seen her?"

"Not since before I bathed," Aiden frowned, worry beginning to peck at him. "Why?"

He started to climb down the hill, but Faralder loped up it instead, his long legs carrying him halfway up in two steps. He scanned the hills and slopes with an uncharacteristically anxious look on his face.

"No one else has seen her, either," Faralder said anxiously. "Jódís sent her home with her grandmother when she went up to do the washing, but the old lady's mind is not what it used to be. Jódís got home and found her mother napping and Agna nowhere to be found. Grandma doesn't remember going home with her at all. We think she might have wandered out into the hills."

Sudden fear gripped Aiden's heart at the thought of the little girl in danger. Agna was no more than six— certainly not old enough to be wandering the hills alone.

"Where's Einarr?" Aiden asked, already scanning the hills as well.

"He's checking around the other spring," Faralder answered, but Aiden was already heading off in the opposite direction of town.

"Tell him I'm going to search the hills for her!"

"You can't go out on your own!" Faralder shouted after him. "We'll lose you both!"

"I used to lose sheep on hills like this all the time!" Aiden plowed ahead, undeterred. "I can handle myself. Tell him to come after me if they find her first!"

"You really are a Galinn!"

Aiden didn't answer, but left Faralder standing on the hill as he hurried off into the foothills.

Chapter Seven

Aiden soon found that, though there were many similarities between the hills and the moor, there were some significant differences as well. Though from a distance, it looked open and flat and inviting, the scrub was dense and thorny in places, and the elevations were far more steep than the peaty fens he was used to. He was soon winded from climbing hill after hill, but he knew someone less experienced would have it far worse. No other creature knew better how to traverse land like this by the easiest path possible than sheep and goats, and Aiden had watched his flock alone enough years to know which way they would go. He followed their imaginary roaming, hoping children, like sheep, would tend to take the path of least resistance, circling around patches of thorny heather and brush and moving down rather than up when they could.

He knew he was heading in the right direction when he spotted a roughly-carved wooden figure dropped in the grass. It was of a six-legged horse, which Einarr said was the fastest horse in the world, and belonged to one of their Gods. It had been Einarr's as a child, carved by his father, and he'd given it to Agna. He bent to pick it up and looked around him, hoping he might spot her. From this far out, the town and the coast were no longer visible. She must be lost, trying to find her way back.

He slipped the horse into his pocket and continued in the direction he'd been going, searching the ground for some sign of her. His heart leaped as he crossed a muddy stream and saw footprints in its bank. They were Agna's size, and continued up the next mossy hill a little ways. The mud was still damp on the grass, splattered on the white flowers. He couldn't be far behind her now. Excitement growing, he hurried up the hill after her.

"Agna!" he called hopefully, "Agni!"

As he reached the top of the hill, he realized how close he was to the mountain now. The outcroppings of rock were getting bigger and more frequent. And near him was a tumble of huge stones that formed a shallow cave. A lost sheep would have headed for just such a place to hide, and Aiden had no doubt Agna had done the same. He hurried toward it, sliding on the rocky scree.

"Agna!" he shouted again as he drew near the cavern, "Agna, it's me!"

He stumbled up to the opening of the cavern, its interior dim and lined with phlox and curling fiddleheads. His worry grew when no one answered him, but he breathed a sigh of relief as he saw her huddled against the cave wall, flowers settled in her hair and about her shoulders, sniffling into her arms.

"Agni," he said, breathless as ducked inside, "Everyone is so worried about you!"

Agna looked up, her eyes full of tears, and threw herself into Aiden's arms, sobbing. Aiden put his arms around her, rubbing her back as she cried herself out, babbling in the Norse language between her sobs. He noticed the swollen bruise on her ankle and winced.

She must have slipped and twisted it, probably on all the shifting, rocky soil near this cavern. He felt bad for her, but at the same time, he hoped it discouraged her from wandering off again anytime soon.

He let her cry a while longer, his eyes on the sun outside the cave. It was past midday by now. Einarr would be frantic.

"We'd better get you home." He stood with her in his arms, stooping to step out of the shallow cavern. "It's going to be late by the time we get back to town. I hope your father hasn't done anything foolish."

Aiden knew Agna could probably only understand one out of every ten words he used, but it made him feel better to talk. He shifted her onto his back, his arms under her legs, and started making his careful way across the loose gravel ridge, looking for a safer way down than the slope that had twisted Agna's ankle. If he fell now, they'd both be stuck out here until someone found them. At least he knew which direction to go.

Taking a safer, more round-about path, he began picking his way back toward home, the going easier now that it was at least mainly downhill. Still, he was soon exhausted, his hands worn bloody from clutching at the heather to keep from slipping, his back aching under Agna's weight.

Suddenly, he heard voices and hope lit like a lantern in him. Einarr and the others must be searching the hills as well! He hurried toward the sound, scrambling up a bank with hands fisted in the damp grass. The men were speaking Norse— no words that Aiden knew— but Agna made a worried sound on his back. Aiden frowned, but kept going until Agna suddenly yanked on his hair. He looked back to see her shaking her head frantically and pointing at the closest cluster of boulders. Something didn't feel right, and Aiden, trusting Agna's instincts, ducked behind the rock. The men were coming this way. If they passed and it was someone Aiden knew, he'd come out, no harm done. And if not...

He crouched behind the rock, watching the bank he'd walked along on his way up. A moment later, three men appeared at the top of it, working their way over the hills in the direction of town. Aiden didn't recognize any of their faces, and they were heavily armed, with no sigil or sign of where they'd come from on their shields of cloaks— or at least none Aiden recognized. Aiden began to think it was a good thing he hadn't run straight into them. Agna clung to him tightly as he began to carefully back away, wondering how he would get around these men to get home.

Agna cried out suddenly, and Aiden turned in surprise to see another two men creeping up behind him. He shouted in surprise and threw a handful of gravel into the nearest man's eyes, then scrambled to run as the second man lunged at him. He swung Agna into his arms as he slid and flailed down the closest hill, but he knew, in this terrain, they'd be caught up to him as soon as he had to slow down to go uphill. He had no weapon. There weren't even any trees here to provide him a good, sturdy stick. He searched frantically for some way out of this situation, panic blossoming like an ugly flower in his heart, stealing his breath and making images of the night his town burned flash before his eyes. He was wheezing with fear, clawing his way up a bank as he looked for somewhere to hide. The five strangers were not far behind him, weapons drawn and shouting words Aiden couldn't understand in a tone that made them all too easy to guess.

He made it over the hill before they caught up and realized he had a few seconds before they reached the top of the hill and saw him again. He squeezed Agna close and looked for a hiding place. There was a rocky overhang— the obvious choice— and a dense thicket of heather. Making a split-second decision, he shoved Agna under the heather, making sure she was hidden by its tangled branches before he turned and ran for the overhang. He crammed himself into the shadowy crevice beneath the stone, praying the strangers would run past both of them.

As the band of strangers appeared over the hill, he realized they would not be that lucky. The men stopped at once, searching the hillside for their quarry. Aiden held his breath, heart battering itself against his ribs, as they moved toward the rocks. If they found him, that would be alright— as long as it kept them from finding Agna. Still, he huddled deeper into his hiding place as they came closer, closing his eyes and hoping against hope that they wouldn't see him.

Suddenly, Aiden heard the sound of the heather rattling and his eyes shot open, his breath catching in his throat. The men turned around at once to investigate the sound, heading toward Agna's hiding spot. Aiden barely even thought before he moved, squeezing out of his hiding place at once, shouting at the men's backs to draw their attention. His back to the rock, he knew he wouldn't be able to run far, but it might buy Agna time to get away. The men turned back toward Aiden at once, one of them swearing irritably in Norse as they readied their swords. Aiden braced himself for the worst even as he was still looking for a way out, for some way to run.

Before he even had time to try and make a run for it— and hopefully lead them further away from Agna— a bellow of rage echoed across the hills as someone launched themselves from the top of the rock Aiden was huddled against. The man closest to Aiden barely had time to register what was happening before Einarr landed with his knees in the stranger's chest and his ax in the man's face. Einarr, seeming to be ten times his normal size with rage, hardly paused to pull his ax free before he'd thrown himself at the next man. By now, the four remaining strangers had recovered from their shock and threw themselves at Einarr as one. Aiden, watching, saw Agna peering from the heather, trying to climb out, and rushed to her past the fighting, ducking the sword of an enemy as it flew past him. Whether it had been swung at him or merely thrown from the hand of someone Einarr was killing, Aiden didn't take time to see. He scooped

Agna up without stopping and just kept running, leaving the bloody scene behind them. He felt his heart screaming at him to go back and help Einarr, but he had no weapon and no skill at fighting. The only way he could help right now was to get Einarr's daughter out of danger so that the other man could focus on staying alive.

After he'd run a good distance, he stopped and looked back, but he could no longer see the place they'd been fighting. Was Einarr alive? The thought of anything else made him cold with fear. Suddenly, he saw the top of someone's head as they crested the hill Aiden had just run down. He held his breath hopefully as the sun caught yellow hair. A moment later, he released it with a sob of relief as Einarr, bloody but alive, came over the hill. The man stumbled down as Aiden hurried toward him, and as they met, Einarr wrapped his arms around Aiden and Agna and squeezed them both to him tightly.

"What were you thinking?" Einarr pressed a breathless kiss to the top of first Agna's head, then Aiden's. "What were either of you thinking?"

"Well, I didn't think there'd be armed bandits wandering around the hills, for one thing," Aiden replied with a laugh tinged by lingering fear.

"Those were no bandits." Einarr released Aiden reluctantly, and from this close, it was easy for Aiden to see what poor shape the man was in. None of his wounds looked fatal, but Aiden knew enough small cuts could kill a man as surely as a stab to the heart. It just took longer.

"We need to get you back to town." Aiden took Einarr's hand, tugging him toward town. "Before you bleed to death."

"We need to see Arnnjorn." Einarr limped after Aiden, his expression stormy with worry. "Those were Jarl Bjorn's men."

Aiden felt a chill, remembering the threat of the Jarl's army. Frightened as he was of it, he had thought they had at least until winter. Einarr saw the fear in Aiden's eyes and stopped abruptly, forcing Aiden to do the same.

"Thank you," said Einarr, still holding Aiden's hand and squeezing it tightly. "I owe you a debt bigger than I can repay. You found my daughter, and you saved her from those men. I saw you reveal yourself to keep them from finding her. You would have died to keep her safe. I would not have expected such bravery from the most hardened of warriors."

Aiden flushed with pleased embarrassment at Einarr's words, shaking his head.

"A hardened warrior would have been able to fight to protect her." Aiden pulled his hand away, flustered. "All I could do was run. And not terribly well, at that."

"You did more than I could." Einarr reached out to catch Aiden's hand again, sliding his touch up to Aiden's elbow to pull the other man closer. Then he leaned down, pressing a kiss to Aiden's cheek. It was warm and somehow made Aiden's heart flutter more powerfully than when they'd kissed in the hot spring. This seemed more tender somehow, driven less by lust than true affection. Aiden blushed hotly and looked away. They said little more as they began walking again, Einarr chatting quietly with the still-sniffling Agna in their own language.

It was early afternoon before they made it back to town. Jódís came running as soon as they appeared at the top of the hill, thanking the Gods and scolding all three of them at the same time in mixed Norse and Welsh. She was nearly in tears as she scooped Agna into her arms. Someone called for Yrsa, who was the best healer in the village, but Einarr refused to see her unless she tended him in the long house while he spoke with Arnnjorn.

Aiden stayed under Einarr's arm, keeping the man on his feet as they limped toward the long house. Einarr pulled a seat up near to Arnnjorn's throne, and the two of them had not been sitting there long before Yrsa the healer arrived, and Arnnjorn close behind her, his hair still wet from bathing.

"Einarr, my brother's son," Arnnjorn said as he hurried to Einarr's side, "What has wounded you in this way? And what could be so dire that you'd take me from my bath at this hour?"

Einarr sat back, pausing for a moment as Yrsa pulled his shirt off and began cleaning out and bandaging his wounds, businesslike and silent.

"My daughter, Agna, wandered out into the hills," Einarr explained. "She says she was looking for flowers and got lost. My thrall, Aiden, learning she was missing, went out to search for her alone. And when I heard of this, I went after them both. Aiden found her, but they were beset by five men carrying many weapons and bearing no banner. As I found them, Aiden had hidden Agna under the heather and was about to give his own life to distract his enemies. He faced them bravely, though he had no weapon and knew it would mean his certain death, had I not appeared at that moment to slay his attackers."

"It's no Midgard serpent." Arnnjorn gave Aiden a look that was part amusement, part respect. "But a brave deed, regardless. It's a worthy thrall you've found, Einarr. But I do not see why this required my immediate attention. If they were bandits, you have dealt with them. Unless you fear there are more?"

"I fear there are many more," Einarr confirmed, wincing as Yrsa cleaned a deep cut on his arm. "I recognized those men's faces. Though they had scrubbed the paint from their shields to hide where they came from, I know they were Jarl Bjorn's men. Or, more likely, Hallvaror Bjornson's men. Jarl Bjorn has never used such tactics."

Arnnjorn inhaled sharply, understanding now, as Einarr continued.

"I believe they were a scout party, or else they had come to sabotage us in preparation for a larger attack. Agna heard them say something about burning boats."

"This is the kind of sneakery I have come to expect of Hallvaror," Arnnjorn agreed, his brow furrowed with grim disappointment.

"Will they use the death of their men as excuse to attack?"

"No, they will deny responsibility, claim the men were outlaws. They need no further excuse than the one they already have. I fully believe their promise to return come winter, when all their men have returned from raiding and the harvest is in. Bjorn is not a man reckless enough to begin a war in the wrong season."

"Then we have time to prepare." Einarr tried to sit up straighter and hissed in pain at the stretch of his injuries. Yrsa tugged him back down with an impatient frown.

"Time to prepare," Einarr continued, grimacing and then leaning forward to look at Arnnjorn seriously, "And perhaps to consider accepting his rule."

"You would have me surrender what has been ours alone for centuries?" Arnnjorn asked, recoiling in offense, but not anger. "Our fathers and forefathers have sat in this hall since the days when the mountains were stones and the Gods still walked among us undisguised."

"Bjorn is an honorable man," Einarr argued. "You have said so yourself. Would bowing to him be so terrible?"

"It would mean the end of what my family has built here," Arnnjorn said, gravely serious. "It would mean the end of our ways. I have heard in the other places that have gone under his banner, he has changed their laws and forbidden the customs he does not care for. People let their stories and rituals fall by the wayside in the name of the roads and walls he has built. It is not worth it. Not at the price of who we are."

Einarr took a deep breath and looked down, searching for the words to argue his point, but Arnnjorn spoke again first, looking at Aiden.

"You know he takes a far less charitable view of thralls. You would not be allowed to go on spoiling this one as you have, fine a servant as he is. Bjorn's thralls are branded and kept in separate houses. He lays their bones in the foundations of his walls to earn the blessings of the Gods."

He looked then from Aiden back to Einarr with an eye of piercing perception.

"And he takes a far dimmer view of ergi than I."

Einarr flinched, then looked up at Arnnjorn, his nostrils flared with sudden, fiery anger. Arnnjorn met his gaze steadily.

"He has set laws against it," Arnnjorn said. "The argr man can be driven out for it, the other fined. And a thrall may be drowned, as an animal is drowned after a man has used it in that way."

Aiden shuddered against Einarr's side, and he knew the other man felt it. He didn't know what ergi or argr were, but he could take a guess.

"You know I have never punished such things," Arnnjorn continued, "Not so long as a man has continued to show himself a man in all other things. Certainly not if he has only enjoyed himself as a man with thralls. But Bjorn may not look so kindly on such things."

The anger in Einarr's expression faded into a worried frown, looking away in thought. His eyes found Aiden's, who stared back at him, unsure which way to encourage him, unsure of his feelings, unsure of everything. Einarr sighed heavily, his shoulders sinking.

"Then we will fight him," Einarr said at last. "But if we fight him, then we must win, or all will be lost regardless."

"We have time," Arnnjorn assured Einarr. "We will be ready."

Arnnjorn started to stand, but Yrsa, still sitting beside Einarr and binding his wounds, held up her hand.

"Wait," she spoke with a soft, commanding voice, "And hear me. Many are the honorable men who have discarded that honor when power and wealth was within their grasp. Do not rely on Bjorn's honor to protect you. Rely less on Hallvaror."

"You are wise, Yrsa." Arnnjorn bowed his head to the healer respectfully. "And close to the Gods. What do you say?"

"Give me a fat ewe." Yrsa tied off the last of Einarr's bandages and stood, solid and powerful as a tree trunk grounded in the earth. "I will take it up to the mountain as a sacrifice and wait for word from the Gods. But until they have spoken, I say get the harvest in and keep the weapons sharp and the ships well-repaired. Jarl Bjorn will not make this an easy fight."

Yrsa was off to the mountains with her ewe even before the sun had set. Arnnjorn began preparations at once on new weapons, shields, and ships, pulling as many men as he dared away from working on the harvest while the others were told to put every spare minute they had into getting ready. The women made plans as well to sew new bandages and blankets and set aside any food they could for a harder winter than usual.

Aiden, Einarr's part done for now, just saw the other man home and into his bed. Jódís was away with the other women, making plans, and she'd taken Agna and her mother with her, reluctant to allow either out of her sight again. Aiden stirred up the fire to keep the house warm as chilly night crept in, and pulled an extra fur over Einarr. As he turned to go, Einarr caught his hand. He was looking at Aiden curiously, different from the desire that had been in his eyes only this morning. Aiden wasn't sure if it was gratitude for Aiden saving Agna, or some realization brought on by realizing how close he'd come to losing Aiden today. Whether it was neither or some combination of both, Einarr didn't seem to know, either. But still, he pulled Aiden down toward him and kissed him, tender and delicate, the barest press of warm lips.

"Share my bed with me tonight." His voice was rough and earnest and set off a flurry of butterflies in Aiden's stomach. His cheeks flushed and embarrassment threatened to freeze his voice in his throat.

"You're injured," Aiden argued, trying to pull away. "You should rest."

"I'm not so injured that you could not lie beside me," Einarr replied, pulling him slowly but insistently back. "I ask for nothing more. I only want to sleep knowing you are beside me, safe and protected."

All the old arguments started warring in Aiden again, but all he said was, "Jódís will see..."

Einarr smiled, his eyes soft and unworried.

"Let me worry about Jódís." He tugged gently, and Aiden followed, allowing himself to be pulled down to sit on the bed beside Einarr. "Her bark is much worse than her bite; I promise. Stay with me."

Aiden swallowed hard, wavering in indecision, but he finally obeyed, lying down next to Einarr, who moved over to give him space and drew the furs up over them. Aiden lay on his side, and Einarr tugged him closer, encouraging the younger man to lay his head on Einarr's bare, bandaged chest. Aiden's heart was racing like a rabbit, but beneath his ear, Einarr's heartbeat was steady and calm, the rush of his breathing as regular and soothing as the crash of surf on the shore. His arm around Aiden was warm and comforting, holding Aiden tight. Aiden still felt the fear of so many things, howling for attention at the back of his mind, but when Einarr was holding him like this, it became easy to ignore them. He felt safe here, where he'd rarely felt safe lately. That was worth whatever price was demanded of him later.

Chapter Eight

The next morning came too soon. Jódís eyed them with disapproval as they woke in the same bed, but she said nothing and handed Aiden his food with less reluctance than usual. After breakfast and washing, Einarr led Aiden outside, but not to the fields. Instead, he took him out to the hills and handed him a shield. Einarr had brought with him his ax and a fine sword. Swords were rare in the village— too expensive for most of the people here to own. Arnnjorn was the only man Aiden knew to have one, and Einarr had this one only because he was Arnnjorn's nephew, and he rarely used it, but kept it hung above the bed in case it was needed.

"What are we doing out here?" Aiden asked, eyeing the weapons warily and weighing the shield he'd been given.

"We're here to teach you how to fight," Einarr replied, still limping, but in good shape despite his injuries. "When Jarl Bjorn's army comes, they will not distinguish between thralls and free men. Every man will need to be able to fight, and I'll be counting on you to defend Agna and Jódís if I fall."

Aiden swallowed nervously, worried by the thought of fighting almost as much as the thought of Einarr dying. But the other man was right— he couldn't just cower and hope Einarr would appear to save him every time he was in danger.

"The first and most important thing you need to learn," Einarr stepped closer and took the shield out of

Aiden's hands in order to fasten it to Aiden's arm instead, showing him carefully where it should sit, "Is how not to get hit. You will not have a chance to fight if you die the first time a sword is swung at you. So, first you will learn the shield. Now, raise your arm."

Aiden, frowning with worry, raised the shield as he was told, making sure it covered his throat and his chest, fairly cowering behind it.

"Well," Einarr said, trying to be encouraging, "That is a good position to protect you from arrow fire. But against an armed opponent, this will not be much good. Here, let me show you..."

They worked for the next few hours, practicing with the shield. When he thought Aiden was ready, Einarr practiced hitting the shield with his ax to show Aiden how it would feel, how he needed to position the shield for each blow, how to dig in his heels, or else get out of the way. By the time they were done, Aiden's arms were sore from holding up the shield, and he felt tired as a dog. He flopped down on the grass, dropping the shield, as soon as Einarr said he could. The other man sat down next to him, breathing a little heavily himself.

"We will do this every day from now until the battle." Einarr reached out to ruffle Aiden's hair. "You will be ready by the time winter comes. A season may not seem like much time, but you will be a trained warrior, ready to defend yourself. I promise."

Aiden wondered privately if being a trained warrior would make any difference when Bjorn came, but he didn't want to spoil the moment.

"Thank you," he said instead. "No one has ever taught me anything like this before. You know I'll do my best to protect everyone."

Einarr smiled, the corners of his eyes wrinkling as he gazed at Aiden with undisguised affection.

"You do seem to have a natural affinity for guarding children," he laughed, sitting back in the grass and groaning a little at the ache of his injuries.

"I'm going to protect you, too," Aiden promised, looking at Einarr seriously. "I have no intention of being left behind."

Einarr looked surprised for a moment before his expression softened into a smile and he pulled the younger man against his side. Aiden leaned against him, nervous, but smiling. Before them, the hills rolled up to the feet of the mountains, turning gold under the sunlight.

"There's one other thing," Einarr said after a moment, reaching into his pocket to pull something out. "I've taken enough away from you. I shouldn't take this too."

He handed Aiden a small bone knife and a piece of soft lime wood a bit wider than Aiden's hand. Aiden ran his fingers over the grain of the wood, caught off guard by the gift.

"I'd hate to see you lose that skill," Einarr smiled as he watched Aiden's reaction. "Not when it was what drew me to you in the first place."

"Thank you, Einarr." Aiden held both gifts tightly, overwhelmed by sudden gratitude. For a moment, he was perplexed by the strangeness of his luck. Surely it had been poor fortune that Arnnjorn's raiders had landed on Aiden's shore— but how much more lucky that, if his village was to be burned, he should be found by someone so kind, who would not only save his life, but give him a new one. In some ways, he felt freer than he'd ever been before the collar was around his neck. In his old village, he could have been killed or driven out for even letting Einarr kiss him that way. Here, if Aiden decided he wanted to, if they dared, they could maybe even... He didn't dare finish the thought, but he turned to hug Einarr gratefully.

"Come on," Einarr said, giving Aiden a squeeze and patting his shoulder briskly. "Let's get going. You didn't think training would get you out of work in the fields, did you?"

Aiden groaned, already tired and sore, but followed as Einarr stood and limped off toward work.

Chapter Nine

The days soon fell into a steady pattern, reliable and surprisingly pleasant. After breakfast with the family, Aiden trained with Einarr behind the house, then went to work on the harvest. Once all the barley and rye was cut, it was baled and dried, then began the tedious work of threshing and winnowing to free the grain from the chaff. After work on the harvest was done for the day, Aiden did what he could to help with the preparations for war. He caulked leaky ships with Faralder, tanned leather for armor with Branulf, sewed blankets and bandages with Jódís who, since his rescue of Agna, seemed to view him more charitably— or at least with less open hostility. The entire village seemed to have warmed to him a little more, and Aiden found himself making friends for the first time in his life. Every day, his attachment to this village and the people in it grew— as did his affection for Einarr.

In the evenings, he worked on his carving after dinner, which they usually had at the mead hall with the whole town, or at home with the family. He'd made a new horse for Agna, and Faralder, seeing his work, had asked Aiden to add a falcon's head to the haft of his ax. At night, he often shared Einarr's bed. He had resisted at first, uncomfortable with lying next to the other man while his family was so close by. But eventually, he gave in and found he'd never slept better than when he was next to the Northman, especially as the nights grew longer and colder.

He'd never stopped to think about love before this— at least, not beyond thinking that it was not something he would ever see. No one would have their daughter marry a bastard, and he was too poor and too disliked to earn affection through money or charm. He'd assumed that was all there was to it, and it was easy not to think about it again. He'd never realized he was unusual for not craving a woman's touch and never becoming excited by the sight of their bodies. But these days, he found himself flushed every time he glimpsed Einarr without his shirt. Now that he was allowing himself to look, he realized how much his eye was drawn to the male form more than the female. Had he always been this way, he wondered? Or was it Einarr's influence that had opened his heart to such things?

Einarr's injuries were mild, and soon healed. It wasn't long after he had his strength back that, as they lay together one night, Aiden felt the man's hands wandering, shifting down Aiden's back to run a thumb over the swell of his hip, then lower to squeeze at his thigh. Aiden looked out from under the furs at the other beds in the house, flushing with embarrassment, but there was only the sound of soft snoring from Jódís and Agna's beds. Einarr's lips found his throat, and Aiden gasped softly at the graze of teeth and tongue against the tender skin there. Einarr's hands pressed at the small of Aiden's back, pulling him closer, and Aiden felt the heat of Einarr's desire. For a moment, he was stiff with nerves, doubts and fears pushing their way in. But as Einarr paused, slowing down to look into Aiden's eyes and run his fingers through the thrall's red hair, Aiden felt his worry disappearing. It couldn't help but melt like spring snow in the face of the deep affection and raw desire in Einarr's eyes.

    Hesitant, but hopeful, Aiden pushed his doubts away and leaned in to kiss Einarr softly, the press of his lips as delicate as the still new feelings growing within him. Einarr held himself back through that tender kiss until he could restrain his feelings no more. He kissed Aiden hard, ravishing the smaller man's mouth like he intended to plunder its treasures. He rolled over on top of Aiden, who was trembling like a bird as Einarr's hands pushed under his tunic to caress his chest. Aiden felt his hips rising almost of their own will, pushing up to rock against the thigh Einarr had pressed between his legs. The heavy furs hung over Einarr's, making a warm and shadowed shelter to hide them as Aiden's shaking hands explored for the first time the powerful muscles of Einarr's chest and shoulders, daring what they'd wanted to for days, learning what another man's body felt like against his fingers while Einarr's fierce kisses stole his breath and left his head spinning.

    He clung to Einarr's shoulders and broke the kiss to stare up at the other man, wide-eyed as Einarr's hand slid between his legs. Red-faced and overwhelmed as Einarr's fingers traced his shape, he almost asked to stop. But then, Einarr's hand closed around him and Aiden's breath and words stopped in his throat. His eyes fluttered as his vision lost focus, squirming as he concentrated on trying to keep his voice from growing too loud. This seemed to amuse Einarr, who only stroked faster, teasing him. Aiden, his heart racing at his own boldness, caught Einarr's head and dragged him down into a heady kiss, muffling his moans against the other man's mouth. Einarr's free hand tangled in Aiden's curls, gripping him almost too tightly in his excitement, in their mutual desperate need to be closer. Einarr let go of Aiden long enough to pull his own shirt out of the way. Aiden gasped in surprise and sudden excitement as he felt Einarr's tool, heavier than his and hot as a brand, sliding against his own. Einarr wrapped his hand around the both of them and Aiden bit his hand to stifle the shout that tried to leave him at the rush of overstimulation as heated flesh ground against heated flesh. He reached down to wrap his hand around them as well, his fingers brushing Einarr's as they fell into time with one another, thrusting into their joined hands. Aiden quaked as the delicious friction overwhelmed him, knowing he wouldn't last.

"Einarr," he whispered, struggling to control his voice, which broke with emotion as he pleaded— for what, he wasn't sure. "Einarr..."

The north man kissed him hard, and Aiden thought, through the haze of orgasm as he spilled his seed across Einarr's hand, that he could hear the other man saying his name as well.

Dazed and trembling, Aiden stared up into Einarr's eyes as their frantic movements stopped. Sudden insecurity crept on him, making him worry he might have ruined the closeness that had been beginning to grow between them, by giving in to this. But Einarr only smiled down at Aiden where he lay breathless and flushed and brushed the hair from his eyes. Aiden wished he could read the look in those eyes better. He saw the affection he'd come to expect, but there was something else there he didn't dare put a name to, lest he was wrong. Instead, he just smiled back, his body still glowing with pleasure, nervous and unsure, but happy, and kissed Einarr again.

Chapter Ten

Arnnjorn had set men to watch the sea and the hills, but either Hallvaror sent no more men, or they saw the sentries and turned back. No complaint was ever sent about the men Einarr had killed, though Einarr kept his ax close at hand anyway, in case their families came looking for retribution. It was mid-autumn when Yrsa the healer came back down from the mountain, looking thin and haggard. It had been a wet and stormy season so far, and the little snow that had fallen had been quickly washed away. The sea was shades of slate gray and deep marble blue beneath the grim, cloudy sky, and Yrsa was an ominous figure in her muddy cloak, making her way down the cold mountain, its sides splashed in red orange trees like splattered blood. She made her way at once to the long house, and Arnnjorn was fetched to come and hear her. All the rest of the town, having been waiting for her return, crowded into the hall as well, anxiously waiting to hear what the Gods had said about their dispute with Jarl Bjorn. Aiden stood beside Einarr, nervously waiting to hear what she would say and how it would affect their preparations. He had been learning about Einarr's Gods, and though he wasn't yet certain he believed in them any more than the Christian God he'd left behind, he knew how seriously everyone here took them. There wasn't a night that passed in the mead hall when stories of the sagas weren't shared. Tales of heroes and Gods—Gods that were surprisingly human to Aiden's eyes, at least compared to the lofty and unknowable God he'd been christened to.

"I have been to the mountain," Yrsa began, speaking loudly and clearly as she pronounced her omen. "I have there made a sacrifice to Odin and asked for his wisdom that we might survive the coming threat. I lay cold and hungry in a cave for many days, and I knew Odin would reward my endurance. As he was hung from Yggdrasil to learn the runes, so was I entombed alone in the mountain to learn the future of our village."

"And what did you see, Yrsa?" Arnnjorn asked, leaning forward in his throne as he waited to hear the verdict of the Gods. "What did they show you?"

"I was given a vision," Yrsa replied. "The army of Jarl Bjorn is coming, and there will be a battle. But it will not be with them."

Murmurs of confusion filled the hall at that, but Yrsa did not flinch, waiting until they were silent again before she continued.

"I saw a great worm— a terrible white dragon— which flew across the waves to our shores, where a golden eagle stood watch. Though it screamed at the dragon with all its fury, it was no match for such a beast. The dragon burned not just through our town, but through all of the northlands. Its breath turned the mountains to glass and left only ash behind it. But then, I dreamed again, and this time, two bears came over the hills and stood beside the eagle, and when they fought together, the dragon was turned away. I can see this to mean only one thing: We must not fight Jarl Bjorn. We must join him, or we will all perish at the hands of the greater enemy that approaches us."

For a moment, there was only silence in the hall as people tried to process what Yrsa had said, but soon, confused and worried voices rose, the beginnings of arguments breaking out. Arnnjorn impatiently held out a hand for silence.

"Who is this new enemy?" he asked. "What else is there to threaten us? Who is the white dragon?"

"I do not know." Yrsa could only shake her head. "Some enemy we have raided against on the English coast, perhaps, or invaders from the far east, or another Jarl, with a larger army than Bjorn. It may not even be a fighting force at all, but some disease or disaster. There is no way to know until it is upon us."

Arnnjorn sank back in his seat, his hand to his beard in deep thought while worried voices grew louder around him again.

"Thank you, Yrsa," Arnnjorn said after a moment. "You have done well. Go now and rest and we will consider your words."

Yrsa bowed to Arnnjorn respectfully, then turned and left, the crowd parting to let her through.

"What shall we do, Arnnjorn?" Einarr asked. "Should we send word to Bjorn of the threat?"

"No," Arnnjorn shook his head, frowning deeply. "No, I will not surrender to the Jarl yet. Not until I see this dragon for myself and know it cannot be beaten."

That evening, Arnnjorn sent out a ship to keep watch further out at sea. From now on, he said, there would be a ship there every day, waiting for the dragon. Meanwhile, preparations for the battle with Bjorn went on, and an air of nervous tension filled the town. It was not their way to sit and wait for an attack, but against an opponent like Bjorn, there seemed little other option.

Aiden, however, found it hard to stay worried. Einarr had a talent for hiding his fears— if he had any at all— and when he smiled at Aiden, or picked him up and swung him around as easily as if he were a child, or kissed him like he'd die without Aiden's breath in his lungs, it was impossible to be afraid. What precisely they were, Aiden didn't know how to put into words. He was Einarr's thrall, and from what he understood, a free man using his thrall in this way wasn't unusual. But Einarr had never treated Aiden as a normal thrall. Somehow, though there was no one he could ask, he knew what they were to each other was not normal; neither did it seem as though their relationship was hated— at least not in this village. Faralder still teased Einarr about it, but no one else brought it up, save for once, when a man called Aiden 'argr' in front of Einarr. Aiden didn't know the word, but whatever it was, it was enough for Einarr to draw his ax, shouting something in Norse and looking angrier than Aiden had ever seen him, until the man apologized to Einarr for whatever the slight had been, and thereafter avoided both of them staunchly. Aiden asked about the word, but Einarr only told him not to worry about it.

The days grew shorter and darker and frigidly cold, the rain storms colder and fiercer, until one day, Aiden woke early to find Einarr not in bed. He pulled on his clothes and found the man standing outside the house. It was still twilight, the sun barely risen, and the world was washed in bright, cold blue. The houses of the village were cobalt shadows standing above the cornflower shore, washed with blue-black waves like ink. An icy snow was spiraling softly out of the endless azure sky, freezing as soon as it touched the ground. Aiden shivered, wishing he'd grabbed a fur before he'd come out here, and reached for Einarr's arm. The man was staring out at the sea, toward where the bright blue melted into orange and pink and gold, a frown on his handsome face. His voice was grim and severe as he spoke the words Aiden could already feel.

"Winter is here."

The next day, they saw banners on the hills in a dozen different colors, all of them bearing the sign of the bear. The full fighting force of all Jarl Bjorn's kingdom— every tribe and clan and village he'd consumed— stood waiting in the hills to descend on the village, or else waiting in the ships just a few miles offshore. The horns woke everyone early, and the women and children were ushered into the hall with the supplies, the door barred behind them. The women were armed, ready to fight if the hall was breached. Aiden watched Einarr hug Jódís and Agna goodbye before they sealed the door, his brave smile slipping for a moment as he hugged Agna tightly and kissed her head.

The men gathered outside the hall, armed and armored to the best of their abilities. Aiden gathered with them, concern filling him at what he saw. There were sixty good fighting men in the village, and they had shields and axes at the least. But the rest were either too poor to afford weapons or otherwise not the kind to go raiding. They clutched wood axes and farming tools and looked pale with fear. Then there were the thralls, who looked most ill-equipped of all. Most of them had never been trained in fighting. None of them owned weapons. Thralls weren't allowed to carry them. Those whose masters had weapons to spare had armed them, but there were not many. Arnnjorn had ordered new weapons made and, though they were crude and hastily put together, they were better than nothing. Aiden assumed he would have one of those as well, since he had no weapon of his own.

Then, Einarr turned to Aiden and pressed his ax into the younger man's hands, followed by his shield, painted blue with a white eagle.

"You trained hard." Einarr smiled proudly. "I trust you to wield these today and protect our family."

Aiden's heart soared at that; at the same time, fear for Einarr's safety filled him. He took the weapons, but his brow was furrowed with concern.

"Won't you need them?" he asked, sliding the shield onto his arm.

"I will use my sword." Einarr pulled it from his belt, holding it reverently. "And I can get another shield. It's more important to me that you are protected."

That sat wrong with Aiden, like a stone in his throat. He shook his head, but he didn't want what might be their last conversation to be an argument. Instead, he reached into his own belt and pulled out a small wooden bead, intricately carved with curling flowers and twisting ivy. As he pulled it out, the blue bead Einarr had given him when they met came out with it.

"I carved this for you," Aiden said, offering it to Einarr, "To replace the one you gave me. And to remind you that I'm going to be waiting for you to come back after this."

Einarr smiled sadly as he looked at the bead, but he didn't reach out to take it, and Aiden knew why. Aiden stepped closer stubbornly and reached out to slide it onto one of the braids of Einarr's beard himself. He tried to ignore the burning tears stinging his eyes.

"We're going to make it through this," Aiden declared, like saying it firmly enough would make it true. "We're going to be safe together at the end of this. Things will be just how they were."

Einarr said nothing, but he reached for Aiden's hand as the younger man finished fastening the bead. He squeezed it once, then opened it to take the blue bead from Aiden's palm. He ran his fingers through Aiden's red curls the way he always loved to, then wove a quick braid into the hair near Aiden's face, securing the blue bead within it.

"So you will remember I'm with you." Einarr's fingers brushed Aiden's cheek as he finished. "And that I'm protecting you."

It wasn't the promise Aiden wanted, but he smiled anyway, wishing he was brave enough to kiss Einarr in front of the other men.

Instead, a horn sounded and they turned with the other men as the watcher Arnnjorn had set on the hills hurried down the slope into the street.

"Jarl Bjorn and Hallvaror Bjornson lead the army," the scout said. "They say they want to speak to Arnnjorn the Red!"

Arnnjorn took a deep breath, steeling himself before he turned to the men.

"They come to offer us one last chance of surrender," Arnnjorn called. "All of us will ride out to meet him, and tell him his offer is refused. Unless there is a dragon on the horizon?"

He did not say this mockingly, but in all seriousness, and turned to Yrsa, who had refused to hide in the hall but stood ready with her bandages and thread to keep anyone she could alive.

"I can only promise you it is coming," she replied. "As surely as the sun rises."

"It's winter, Yrsa." Arnnjorn's voice was grave and worried. "The sun will not rise again until spring."

Yrsa said nothing, but stood firm as a planted stone, certain as ever in her vision.

"Prepare yourselves," Arnnjorn called, turning to his men again, "Bjorn may outnumber us, but we know this land. It has been ours a thousand generations. It will defend us. Fight like furies, and do not go easily into the halls of Asgard— at least not without ten of Bjorn's host riding beside you!"

The men cheered ferociously and began to move up the hill toward where Bjorn's army was waiting. Aiden went with them, staying close to Einarr's side. They had barely begun when, suddenly, a voice called out.

"Wait! Wait, Arnnjorn! A ship! It's the sentry!"

Arnnjorn turned back at once as the ship, rowing as fast as it could, rammed directly into the harbor without slowing. The two men in it leapt out, scrambling to get to Arnnjorn with their news.

"Fire, down the coast!" one said. "And ships, fleeing the destruction!"

"Women and children," said the other. "They say a huge force is sailing up the coast burning any settlement they see!"

"It's the English." The first man, shaken, stared at Arnnjorn with wide eyes. "I know not which king, but they intend to destroy us!"

"All the villages down that coast are under Bjorn's banner." Arnnjorn's hand went to his beard again, sympathy in his eyes. "And all his men are at our doorstep. He has left no one behind to guard them. I have never known Bjorn to be such a fool. I know he does not think we are such a threat that he needed every man. That son of his must have convinced him if we saw the size of his army, we would surrender without a fight."

"There's your dragon." Yrsa appeared at Arnnjorn's side, her expression grim. "Will you do what I asked you now, if it is not too late?"

Arnnjorn bowed his head.

"Forgive me for not heeding your council better, wise Yrsa." Arnnjorn shook off his shame and turned to the sentries. "Where are the survivors' ships going?"

"The colonies in Northumbria," the sentries replied. "We asked them to follow us back, at least for supplies, for they were wounded and under prepared, but they refused. They say the English ships are coming here next."

Aiden, already pale, pressed close to Einarr's side at that, anxiety churning in his gut.

"Bjorn will want to hear of that." Arnnjorn turned toward the hills again. "If Yrsa's vision holds true and we survive this, he will need to send men after them."

He said no more, but turned toward the hills again. His men hesitated, wondering if they should follow, but when they moved to do so, Arnnjorn held up a hand to stop them. He went alone out onto the hill. Aiden and the other men all hurried to stand where they could see the distant, imposing figures of Bjorn and Hallvaror on horseback before their vast army. Arnnjorn seemed very small in comparison as he went to stand in front of them.

Aiden wished he could hear what was said, but he could only watch, bracing himself always for violence. But it appeared Arnnjorn was at least as skilled a diplomat as he was a leader of warriors. After they had spoken for a while, Aiden released a breath he hadn't realized he'd been holding when Bjorn and Hallvaror turned away from Arnnjorn and back toward their men. Arnnjorn turned as well, hurrying back toward them across the hills.

"They have been told of the coming threat," Arnnjorn said as he approached, "And they will fight with us here. The terms of our surrender to their rule will be decided after the battle is won or lost."

Aiden could see how much it pained Arnnjorn to be giving up this way, but he admired the man's strength in pushing past his pride to save his people. He could tell not all his people felt the same. It was the nature of the northmen to prefer to die fighting rather than surrender for the sake of a chance at survival. But Yrsa's prophecy loomed large in everyone's memories. It was one thing for their village to be lost, another to allow the English to wipe out all heathen kind.

The men dispersed to wait for sign of English sails on the horizon. Bjorn's army camped outside of town while Bjorn and his son joined Arnnjorn in the long house to talk strategy. The women and children were, for now, still staying within the hall as well. They couldn't be sure how quickly the English would appear, and there might not be time to herd everyone in again. Many of the men went there to listen to the war talk and be with their families, but Einarr went home, and Aiden followed him.

"Don't you want to see Agna?" Aiden asked curiously as Einarr paused outside the house, running his hand over the carvings on the mantle his father had done.

"I couldn't bear to say goodbye to her again," Einarr explained, still looking lingeringly at the carvings before, at last, he moved inside, leaving the door open for Aiden to follow. Aiden hesitated for a moment, looking back at the heavy, steel gray sky, just waiting to pour out a miserable storm on their heads. But for now, everything was silent, tense with anticipation of the coming blow.

Inside, Aiden found Einarr packing a bag.

"What are you doing?" Aiden was understandably confused, reaching out a hand to stop Einarr. "Are you planning on running?"

If he was, Aiden would go with him, but that wasn't the Einarr he knew. He certainly wouldn't go anywhere without Agna and Jódís.

"No," Einarr explained, pausing only for a moment. "This is for you."

"Why?" Aiden, baffled, caught Einarr's hands to stop the man again. "Do you think I can't fight them? You were confident when I was going to fight Bjorn's army."

"It's not that," Einarr hurried to clarify, taking Aiden by the shoulders. "It's me. I did this to you. I burned your home, brought you here, and forced all of this on you. You might have lived a long and happy life if I had not been so determined to have you. Now, you could die here, and it would be entirely my doing. But these are your countrymen. You might still have a chance. If you flee now, you could go to them when they land, and they could take you back to your homeland."

Aiden listened to all of this, aghast, and hurt that Einarr had so misunderstood his feelings.

"I don't want to go back there." Aiden's eyes flashed with anger and determination. "I want to be here. I want to be with you. You may have brought me here against my will, but you gave me a better life than I ever had when I was free. I have been truly happy here for the first time in my life."

His heart raced as he spilled out his feelings, only now realizing they were true. What he hadn't yet had the courage to admit to himself fell from his lips of its own accord.

"I love you, Einarr." Aiden reached up to hold Einarr's face in his hands. "Those aren't my people any more, and that isn't my home. My home is wherever you are. And I won't let that be taken away again. For longer than I can remember, I've just been resigning myself to whatever life was given to me, accepting it as the best I could have and never fighting for anything more. But I want this. I want to be here with you. I'm not just resigned, and I'm willing to fight and die to stay here if I need to. I love you."

Einarr was silent for a moment, and Aiden was afraid the other man would argue, insist Aiden try to run. But Einarr just wrapped his arms around Aiden and pulled him close into a bruising, powerful kiss, which Aiden returned just as desperately. Before he knew it, they had fallen into the bed, pulling at one another's clothing. Aiden's fear of this had vanished. God could damn him if he liked. There was no way Aiden would rather spend these last moments than like this. Heaven could burn— he would follow wherever Einarr went when the end came.

Their hands were rushed and clumsy, forgetting skill in favor of simply getting as close to each other as they could in the time they had left, with no idea how long that would be. Einarr pushed Aiden's tunic up to shower his chest and stomach with kisses, murmuring adoring words, worshipping the man underneath him like some new God of ecstatic pleasure. But Aiden wanted to worship as much as be worshipped. His hands tangled in Einarr's hair, caressed his jaw, and ran over his shoulders and chest, learning all of his angles with frantic passion, in case this was his last chance and he'd need to remember every corner of the other man forever from nothing but this. Aiden wanted to be able to see every inch of Einarr with his eyes closed.

Einarr pulled Aiden's pants down and Aiden gasped in relief as, already swollen and sensitive, he sprung free from the tight cloth. Einarr kissed the blushing head of his tool as he wrapped his hand around the shaft. Aiden, for once, didn't have to restrain his voice, moaning throatily as Einarr touched him. Einarr chuckled a little at that, looking up at Aiden lovingly.

"You're so noisy," he chuckled. "You've been trying too hard to stay quiet all this time, haven't you?"

He leaned up to kiss Aiden, who was too flustered to respond to the teasing.

"Don't hold back," Einarr whispered against Aiden's lips. "I want to hear how much you want me today."

He didn't need to wait long to hear Aiden's voice as he squeezed the smaller man in a tight stroke. A moment later, he felt Einarr's fingers against his entrance and gasped, face flushing darkly. Einarr had begun touching him there more recently, shameful as Aiden felt it must be. He kept a small container of oil near the bed, and he reached for it now, pouring a little on his fingers and rubbing slow circles around Aiden's hole, stroking him with his other hand. Aiden covered his eyes in embarrassment, sprawled in utter disarray, his tunic pushed up over his chest, his face flushed, his eyes hazy, and his red hair curling across the silver fur they lay on, his bare and slender hips in Einarr's lap as the older man's fingers pressed into him. Aiden couldn't deny he enjoyed the feeling, strange as it was. The skin there was almost more sensitive than anywhere else on his body, and the feeling of being stretched open and filled up was oddly satisfying. And when Einarr's fingers moved just the right way... Aiden gave a high, keening cry as Einarr found the spot that sent white hot waves of pleasure through him, surging up his shaft until he throbbed and dripped with pleasure. Every press there felt like an orgasm in miniature. Embarrassing as it was to have someone touch him this way, he craved it. It was no wonder he'd been so unhappy before, barely daring to touch himself for fear of divine retribution, when this had been inside him all along just waiting to be found.

Suddenly, just as he thought he was about to cum, Einarr pulled his fingers away and Aiden whimpered at the loss, almost demanding they be put back. Instead, he opened his eyes as Einarr moved to lean over him. He thought the man was going to kiss him, but instead Einarr only leaned closer to stare into Aiden's eyes. Aiden, panting and breathless, stared back, awed by the overflowing emotion he saw there. He felt small and petty in the sight of such passion. If that was love, then Aiden had felt only the barest corner of it. He wanted to be that full of love— wanted to make Einarr feel as loved as he did now, but he didn't know how. Einarr closed his eyes and pressed his forehead against Aiden's, just lingering in closeness as long as he could.

"I love you too, Aiden," he said at last, his voice shaking like saying the words frightened him, like he was scared of how deeply he meant them, and how far he would go to prove them. "I love you."

Aiden trembled like the emotions were too much for him to bear and would burst out of him like light. He caught Einarr by the back of the head and kissed him again, wishing he had the power to fill that kiss with all the things he felt, but couldn't put into words. What had started as an imprisonment and become a fragile, unnamed pleasure was blossoming into something new, real and lasting. Aiden felt that, if he loved Einarr this much when they were only just now beginning, how great and terrible a love it might become with time. He might, one day, even begin to match the adoration he saw in Einarr's eyes.

Einarr's hands caught his thighs and Aiden shivered as he felt the brand of Einarr's tool pressing against his entrance. He braced himself, tensing for it, but Einarr didn't push forward yet. He rubbed a hand over Aiden's stomach instead, murmuring quiet, soothing words until Aiden relaxed, taking deep breaths. Finally, he moved, sliding in. Aiden's spine bowed, sucking in a long breath as he opened up for the other man. It burned. His legs over Einarr's shoulders flexed and stretched as he bit down and tried to bear it, pushing through to the pleasure beyond the sting. Because there was pleasure there in the pressure and the fullness, in the weight against the place that sent sparks dancing behind his eyelids.

Einarr took his time, slowly filling Aiden to the limits of what he could take, until he was shaking like a leaf, breath quick and labored. He felt like he was melting from his core, overheated with exertion and arousal. Einarr's hands were on his hips, and Aiden clung to his wrists, stopping him for a moment while he tried to make it through the overwhelming rush of sensations. Einarr let go of his hip in order to lace his fingers with Aiden's, holding him in place like an anchor when the feelings threatened to sweep him away like a tidal wave. Gradually, Aiden adjusted, his frantic heart slowing, his breath evening out. Einarr lifted Aiden's hand to kiss it, and even that little motion made Aiden groan and realized he wanted more— as much more as he could take. He looked at Einarr with hazy, unfocused eyes, the blue bead glittering in his hair marking him as Einarr's more than the collar around his throat ever could.

"Are you ready?" Einarr asked, holding Aiden's hand to his face.

Aiden nodded, wordless with thought-scrambling overstimulation, his finger tracing Einarr's cheekbone as delicately as the brush of a feather.

Einarr smiled, turned his head to kiss Aiden's palm, and then began to move, rocking slowly deeper in, only to retreat like the tide, every swell building toward the storm. As he began to move faster, he pushed against the place inside of Aiden that his fingers had found before and set fire to Aiden's nerves, lighting him up from the roots of his hair to the tips of his fingers. He couldn't hold back from moaning Einarr's name every time, and soon, he was rolling his hips back against Einarr's thrusts, needing more of him, needing him deeper.

Nothing beyond that room mattered. The English could have stormed the village at that moment, and neither of them would have cared. Everything they wanted was right there between them. Aiden felt like he could lose himself to this so easily. He could forget the whole world and every other ambition he'd ever had just to lay in this bed with Einarr over him forever.

His body rocked, and the wooden bench creaked beneath them. He could hear thunder rumbling outside, and see dust rising into the light from the fervor of their motions, surrounding them in a halo of drifting gold. Pleasure washed over him in waves that left him senseless and gasping, unable to get his bearings before the next wave hit and left him dizzy and keening for more again. Einarr's face was intent, focusing on Aiden like he was all that existed, or like he wanted to hold onto this image of him forever— to be certain it was exactly like this when he reached paradise.

"Einarr," Aiden found words at last as he felt a coil tightening in his belly, the pleasure growing too intense to hold onto. "Einarr, I'm almost..."

Einarr moved faster in reply, driving into him deeper and harder and giving Aiden no choice but to tumble over the edge into overwhelming ecstasy. Einarr followed him a few thrusts later, burying himself as deeply within the other man as he could before he spilled his seed, warm and strange inside Aiden. Einarr bent and wrapped his arms around Aiden, lifting him up to sit in Einarr's lap. Einarr was still inside him, still throbbing with the last moments of orgasm, and he needed Aiden closer, pressed against his chest. Aiden, his toes curling with the lingering aftershocks of pleasure, clung to Einarr and pressed kisses to his throat, vision swimming as Einarr held them tightly together.

Later, when they'd cleaned one another and lay in the furs beside each other, Aiden experienced a deep, warm contentment he'd never known before. If things ended today, at least he'd experienced this. He'd seen adventure, he'd become part of a community that valued him and wanted him around. He'd fallen in love and felt pleasure he couldn't have imagined— all things he'd never dared to hope for in his old life. He wanted more, so much it ached, and he was going to fight for the chance to have a life with Einarr. But if that wasn't what destiny had in mind for him, if this was all the happiness that had been portioned for him, it was more than he'd expected, and he was grateful for it. Einarr was holding his hand, had lifted it up to examine his fingers like they were something marvelous. His smile was as genuine as Aiden had ever seen it, hiding nothing. He was, as Aiden, lingering in perfect happiness, while distant thunder grew closer.

Chapter Eleven

    Their reverie was interrupted by the sound of horns. They looked at each other, worry replacing their content warmth as they realized what it meant. They hurried to their feet and pulled their clothing back on as quickly as they could, checking to make sure they had their weapons and were ready to fight. They kissed each other one last time in the doorway, lingering and heated, and then hurried out into the crowd of other men gathering at the hall again. Arnnjorn stood there, and Hallvaror stood beside him, blond and smug as ever, though there was an air of severity to him now that didn't suit his handsome face.

    "Bjornson will take a part of his father's army in our boats and their own out to meet the ships," Arnnjorn was explaining as Aiden and Einarr arrived, running to stand beside Faralder and Branulf. "They will board and attempt to take control of them. If any of the ships land, we are to meet them. We organize ourselves along this road and try to funnel their forces through the town and into the hills where Jarl Bjorn is waiting with the bulk of his force. We drive them into his army and pen them in. We must get them out of the village as fast as possible, before they have time to do any damage or, Gods forbid, reach the long house. Take courage. Where before we were sixty or seventy men going into a battle, ready to die, now we are near two hundred men, facing a fight we can win."

    The men cheered, and Einarr turned to Branulf.

"How close are they?" he asked. "Do we know yet?"

"From what was said, their ships are fast." Branulf looked out at the horizon with a frown. "Not as fast as a longboat, but fast. We should be seeing their sails any moment. Are you ready?"

"As ready as I can be," Einarr agreed.

"Of course, he's ready!" Faralder said, grinning. "He's a northman! We're always ready to die! Live every moment like it's your last and go to Valhalla laughing!"

He gave a whoop of laughter, excited for the battle ahead and the chance for an exalted death. He shook Aiden by the shoulder.

"Even this little Geilir is ready! He's been throwing himself in front of blades since we met him!"

"Geilir, that's a new one," Aiden observed. "What does it mean?"

"Fiery," Einarr provided. "I think it suits you. I like it."

"Geilir, it is!" Faralder agreed loudly, and Aiden found himself smiling in spite of everything.

"You could just call me 'Aiden,'" he suggested, but Faralder scoffed.

"Where's the fun in that?"

"Sails," Branulf interrupted them, pointing out at the horizon, where the white sheets of English-style ships were sailing toward them. Hallvaror had already climbed into a longboat with his men, and it was joined by all of Bjorn's ships and all of Arnnjorn's as well.

Aiden watched them sail out, nerves jangling like metal in his ears, and wished he could hold Einarr's hand. He shook it off, knowing he needed to look strong and face this bravely.

Seven ships sailed over the horizon, their flags bright and their sails pure white. They would be brighter soon, Aiden knew, when Hallvaror's ships reached them and set them alight.

Arnnjorn began ordering the men into position, some on the beach with a shield wall to greet the enemy, others prepared along the path they'd chose to force the men along.

A fog was rolling in, and the thunder grew ever louder. The ocean was a broken mirror, jagged waves crashing on the dark surface. Arnnjorn looked at the weather with satisfaction.

"The Gods are with us," he said. "We have their blessing! Do not let them down!"

A moment later, the fog was lit by the first of the English ships erupting into flame. The men cheered raucously, but Aiden watched in tense silence, hoping that was not the only ship that would burn before it landed. As the fog swallowed the beach, it became impossible to tell. There were no lights on in the village, making this fog deadly to a ship in unfamiliar water. When Arnnjorn heard the creaking of sails and wood, he hollered at the men to get away from the beach. They backed away quickly and, a moment later, the English ships were beaching themselves on the shore, bursting their hulls as they crashed directly into the village docks.

"Brace yourself." Einarr got his shield in position, as did the other men, though Aiden was still reeling from the sight of the huge ships crashing. But he did as he was told, and sure enough, a moment later, the English were streaming from the broken ships, screaming as they came. Aiden gripped his ax hard, and a second later, the men rushed forward to meet the enemy with screams of their own.

Aiden had planned to stay near to Einarr, but he soon lost track of the other man and knew he couldn't afford to focus on anything but surviving. At first, he saw nothing but the men around him, rushing forward in frothing, blood-hungry excitement. Then blood, hot and stinking, splattered across his face as someone shoved a pike through the man in front of him. Suddenly, his ears were open to the sound of screams and metal ringing around him. He threw himself at the soldier who'd murdered his friend, swinging his ax on pure instinct and catching the stranger under the chin. He felt more blood, and a rush of simultaneous horror and joy. He'd taken a life. He had that power now. He could fight for the life he'd chosen.

He found his back not to Einarr's, but to Faralder's, lashing out at any enemy that dared approach from the chaos around them. Faralder whooped and howled with delight at every swing of his ax and shouted his pride at Aiden's ferociousness. But then, the tides changed and they were separated, and Aiden saw Branulf on the ground, pinned by two men. Branulf had his shield up, the enemies knelt on it, trying to stab at Branulf around it. Aiden didn't think twice before throwing himself at them, killing one and knocking the other away, guarding Branulf until he could get to his feet and take care of the second man himself. They said nothing to each other— just jumped back into the fray.

Aiden lost track of time, lost track of how many enemies he'd killed, lost track of everything in the chain of people he needed to protect. But after a time, he realized something was wrong. The enemy were not moving up toward the hills the way they were supposed to. Arnnjorn's men were holding their own well, but more Englishmen were coming from the three boats that had made it to shore every minute. If they didn't get the enemy moving soon, they would be overwhelmed. His eyes darted across the chaos, shouldering his way past men he recognized and taking his ax to those he didn't, searching for Arnnjorn.

He found the massive, redheaded chieftain a few minutes later, engaged in furious battle with a tall, dark-haired man. From the quality of his clothes and his sword, it didn't take much for Aiden to guess that the man was, at the very least, the captain of one of these ships. If Arnnjorn baited him, Aiden knew the men would follow, but Arnnjorn seemed fixed on defeating the man himself. Aiden hesitated. Arnnjorn knew what he was doing. To interrupt him would not be wise. But as another English warrior knocked Arnnjorn away, Aiden realized the rules of battle were not like that. He darted in, using his small size to his advantage as he ducked other enemies and locked combatants. He appeared in front of the English captain before the man had even finished reeling from the fight with Arnnjorn. He lashed out with his ax recklessly, not aiming to kill, and saw the captain recoil in shock at the ruthless attack, which slashed open his face and left him bleeding. The man gave a shout of anger and pain and ran at Aiden, who'd moved back as quickly as he moved in. Aiden led the man backwards, darting in to jab at him again every few steps, but taunting him always back, down the village streets toward the hill. He leapt onto a barrel as he got too far ahead of his target, in order to shout slurs in his direction. He could see the other warriors moving, following their captain as he charged through the village. Aiden grinned proudly, and for a moment, he glimpsed Einarr through the chaos, bloody but alive and fighting. Aiden raised his ax, pride and exultation shining through him.

Then, something hit him in the chest, hard as a hammer it felt, knocking him from the barrel. As he tumbled toward the ground, he could see the happiness in Einarr's face shift to horror. He tasted blood and smelled earth as he fell into the mud. Above him, the clouds broke open and poured a furious storm down on the world.

Chapter Twelve

He woke up, which surprised him.

He was lying in the mead hall, and Yrsa, scarred and tired, but alive, was leaning over him, cleaning a wound in his right shoulder, which felt like it was on fire with pain. He groaned miserably.

"Oh, good." Yrsa didn't look up from her work, but she smiled. "You're alive. If you're conscious now, you will probably pull through. Congratulations."

"Einarr?" Aiden asked immediately, fear gripping his heart.

"Beside you," Yrsa scoffed a little at that. "He refused to leave your side, so I had to tend to his wounds next to you."

Aiden looked to his left and sighed with relief when he saw Einarr lying on furs beside him, breathing evenly in his sleep. He didn't seem badly hurt, though he was bandaged. Agna was curled up under his arm, asleep as well.

"Are the English gone?" Aiden asked. "What happened?"

"Be patient." Yrsa rolled her eyes. "You're in no danger, and you'll know in a minute."

Aiden frowned, but it did seem like something was happening. The hall was full of injured men being treated by the women, and dead men waiting for burial. Aiden was relieved to see no overly familiar faces among them. They'd lost many, but everyone Aiden loved was still here. The village was still here.

Arnnjorn stood near the end of the hall with Bjorn and Hallvaror. Hallvaror was heavily injured, barely standing, but was insisting on being part of the talks, anyway. Aiden had never seen Bjorn this close yet. He was a tall, somber man, gray as the steel of his weapon, severe and grim. He had the aura of a man who considered honor above all things.

"What kind of king would I be," Bjorn was saying, "If I turned against the men I just fought beside? If you say to come under my banner would be to give up your freedom, then I will not make thralls of free men. You will remain independent, on the condition that you remain my allies. I will want your warriors to fight and raid beside me again one day."

"You have a deal," Arnnjorn agreed with a smile, though Hallvaror looked put out. Bjorn ignored his complaints.

Aiden's heart lifted with hope. They had made it. They had more than survived. They had won.

Later, they gathered the spoils of their victory in the hall to be divided. Aiden, from his place on the floor where he was being made to rest and heal next to Einarr, watched as they carried in weapons and armor and goods taken from the beached ships. The man whose face Aiden had scarred must have been nobility, because his ship had been quite extravagantly appointed with silver and gold furnishings. *What vanity*, Aiden thought, amused. *Maredudd would disapprove.*

Aiden knew enough Norse now that, when Arnnjorn stood and spoke over the bounty, he understood the words.

"Now is time for the bestowing of treasure," the redheaded chieftain declared, "And for the telling of deeds. Faralder, your family is the largest in the village, so the largest portion goes to you. Have you any deeds to declare?"

"Not for myself, Arnnjorn," Faralder said with a grin, glancing at Aiden. "But I would declare deeds for one too modest to speak of them himself."

Arnnjorn held his hand up to make Faralder pause.

"There is no need for your tale spinning today, Faralder," Arnnjorn laughed, shaking his head. "For I have seen his deeds myself. Though I am certain your version of them would be more elaborate. Thrall Aiden, stand."

Aiden stared for a moment, caught off guard, then glanced nervously at Einarr and stood, reminded of his first night here. His wound complained, but his legs still worked. He steadied himself on a pillar.

"You'll have your first battle scar from that." Arnnjorn nodded to the injury. "And it was well-earned. Though you were brought here only a little more than a season ago, you have earned your place well through hard work and unwavering bravery. From your battle with the Midgard serpent—"

He paused to wink playfully at Faralder.

"To your valor in the rescue of Einarr's only daughter. And this night, you have thrice proved yourself the equal in courage of any warrior here. Though your skills are crude, you never hesitated or retreated, but threw yourself into harm's way a dozen times to save the men who you once called your captors. And when even I could not defeat the English captain, who had slain a score of us already, you ran into him without fear and led him and all his army into the trap we had set for them. You burned like a fire in the heart of the battle, Aiden Geilir, and when the Gods thought you were extinguished, the sky wept and sent your soul back to us. We have selfishly withheld you from Valhalla tonight, and I hope you can forgive us."

"I think I can live with that," Aiden replied, and laughter briefly filled the hall.

"For your bravery," Arnnjorn continued, "I wish to give you a great reward."

He reached into the bounty and pulled out two heavy gold rings. Aiden's eyes widened as Arnnjorn brought them to him and pressed one into his hands.

"These rings were on the fingers of the English chief. It seems only appropriate that you should have one. The other, I give to your owner, Einarr, who struck the killing blow to the chief's heart, defending your body when you fell."

He handed the other to the still-seated Einarr, who grinned at Aiden, glowing with pride.

Arnnjorn started to turn away, but Aiden called out to him.

"Um, sir," he said, unsure even after all this time how to address the man. "Can I ask— I was told once that a thrall can buy their freedom. How much do I cost?"

Arnnjorn turned back, surprised, but he smiled broadly at the question.

"A male thrall is worth eight aurar of silver," Arnnjorn said, "Or one of gold."

"Would this be enough?" Aiden asked, holding up the ring, "I have a little more silver, too, probably two ounces. I don't know if that's the same as aurar..."

"It is more than enough." Arnnjorn gave a pleased nod. "And I will be very glad to welcome you to the ranks of my warriors when you are a free man."

Einarr, who had risen behind him, threw his arms around Aiden and hugged him tightly, laughing as a celebration erupted around them. As soon as the bounty was finished being divided, the victory celebration began, which served as the celebration for Aiden's freeing as well. As was the custom, Aiden sat at Einarr's feet and served him one last time, bringing him food and drink through the night. Einarr's hand stayed in his hair any time Aiden was beside him, and once or twice, well-supplied with mead, he dared to steal a kiss. There was no outcry from the other men as Aiden feared there would be. Faralder only laughed when he saw it. Aiden saw no loss of respect in anyone's eyes as he'd expected. It seemed as though they'd known all along and simply didn't care. So long as they went on proving their strength and courage in raids and battles, what they did behind closed doors seemed not to matter. Aiden felt dizzy with happiness, as well as mead.

At last, he knelt in the center of the room while Einarr, with a pair of metal tongs, broke the iron collar around his neck. Aiden saw it fall into the dust like a weight falling from his shoulders and shivered with delight.

"Stand, Aiden of Arnnstead," Arnnjorn called. "You knelt a slave, and stand a free man. We welcome you into our home as an equal."

Aiden stood and turned to face Einarr, who reached out to hold Aiden's face, looking into his eyes in undisguised adoration. He pulled Aiden into a tight hug as the men around them cheered and the music started up again. Squeezing Aiden close enough that his breath brushed Aiden's ear, he spoke.

"I love you," he said. "I will always love you. Now that you're free, you are no longer bound to me. If you choose to leave, I cannot make you stay. But Gods above, I hope you stay."

Aiden pulled away so that he could see Einarr's eyes, reaching up to touch his cheek.

"Where would I go?" he asked. "My home is right here, next to you. I love you too, Einarr. You may not own me any longer, but I will be yours forever."

Chapter Thirteen

Within a few weeks, winter had mellowed. Though Aiden's injury still bothered him, he was mostly on his feet again— not that there was much to do at the moment. True winter had fallen, and with it, enough snow to nearly bury the village. Most days, there was little to do but lie at home among the furs, which Aiden hardly resented while he was healing, and especially not when those furs were so often shared by Einarr.

They stood in the doorway one morning, in that blue twilight hour before the sun had risen, wrapped in a silver fur and in each other. Aiden's back was pressed to Einarr's chest, the other man's arms warm around him, and a welcome shield against the chill. The light dyed the endless, smooth blanket of white snow a soft blue, pristine and familiar now. Aiden could barely remember his life before he'd come here. All he knew was that it was an endless, grinding wheel of lonely misery he was relieved to have left behind. Whatever happened now, he was resigned to nothing. This was the life he wanted, the life he'd chosen, and the life he'd fight to keep.

"In the spring," Einarr said, "When we begin the planting, Faralder wants you to work on the boats with him."

"He told me," Aiden sighed contently, leaning back against Einarr. "He wants me carving mastheads. I think I'll enjoy it, actually."

"Before you grow too busy with Faralder, I want to ask you for a carving of my own."

He turned a little to touch the door frame, carved by his father.

"I would like you to add to the mantle." He ran his hands over those carvings with a fond smile. "These are my father's achievements— his hopes for the future. I want to see our future there now. This is your home now. You should have your mark on it."

"My home already wears my carvings," Aiden smiled, touching the pendant and the bead Einarr still wore. "But I'll think of something, if you like."

Einarr smiled and kissed the side of Aiden's head. Aiden looked back out over the landscape as the wind swept flurries of snow across the banks, swirling and diaphanous as a lady's scarf.

"I hear Arnnjorn is making plans for your future, as well," Aiden said after a moment. "Is it true he's making you his heir?"

Einarr took a deep breath before he answered.

"I believe he is. I am his nephew. But I always thought he was still young enough to have a son."

"Perhaps he believes he already has one," Aiden suggested, and Einarr smiled.

"Things may change if I'm made chieftain," Einarr warned him, turning Aiden to look him in the eye. "But please believe one thing will never change. I will never stop loving you. I will love you more every day until the day I die, and that is a vow."

Aiden's heart throbbed, and he wrapped his arms around Einarr, hugging him tightly.

"I love you too, Einarr. Forever."

Beyond them, the blue horizon lit up with gold as the sun began to rise, turning the sea brilliant jade and sapphire and sparkling like diamonds on the snow that covered the village like a blanket. Spring would come, and changes would come with it, but for now, the world was at rest— in perfect peace— and Aiden was alive, and every day happier than he'd ever been before. Perhaps God did exist, albeit one far different from the cruel spirit Maredudd had preached. Or, perhaps it was Einarr's Gods who were true. Something certainly had heard his prayers all those months ago as he lay in his bed, hollowed out by tedious misery. They'd sent him through fire, only to hand him everything he'd ever longed for and never dared to ask for on the other side. He was reminded of Yrsa's trial in the cave, and her story of Odin hanging on a tree. Perhaps it was Odin who had heard him then, and demanded Aiden fight for the happiness he wanted. That seemed right. Whatever spirits watched and guided, if there were any at all, Aiden was forever grateful to them.

As the sun rose higher, Einarr led Aiden back into the still sleeping house to begin the day, and Aiden cast a lingering glance back at that golden horizon. Truly, the future looked as bright as the sunlight, chasing away the blue shadows of twilight. And whatever further challenges or sacrifices it demanded of him, Aiden would not face them alone. He turned and followed Einarr in, happy at last.

Made in the USA
San Bernardino, CA
25 April 2017